Carol L. Craig

The Great Unraveling

© 2020 by Carol Craig
Published by Ingram Spark
1 Ingram Blvd.
La Vergne, TN, 37086

Printed in the United States of America.

Titles may be purchased in bulk for educational, business, fundraising, or sales promotional use. For more information, contact Carol Craig @ www.editinggallery.com.

Library of Congress Cataloging-in-Publication Data

Craig, Carol, 1957-
    The Great Unraveling / Carol Craig.
      p. Cm. – Historical women's fiction
    ISBN 978-163625231-5

Edited by Sara Rolat
Cover designed by Darrin Brenner: D. Brenner Art & Design

Printed in the United States of America
09 10 11 12 13 RRD 7 6 5 4 3

"They say that a single thread carries the weight of the fabric. Pull on that thread and you can unravel the world. And so it was, on a hot muggy July day, Lydia McAllister unwittingly pulled on that thread, fraying the edges of the pattern she'd woven for her life. Soon, her world would begin unraveling and everything with it.

But I'm getting ahead of myself..."

From the novel, *The Great Unraveling*, by Joan Elaine Fields, M.D.
Based on the diary entries of Rose Watson

1

"In the textile industry, gauze examiners, warpers, twisters, and plugwinders were mostly female. They were brought in from farms, thereby transforming the rural labor market. Barges gave way to trains in transporting materials to market. Even the system by which cotton was grown and purchased changed as a result of the Civil War and the loss of the plantation system and slavery. Females provided cheap labor, while at the same time giving the women their first taste of independence. Many men saw it as the unraveling of society, whereas many women saw it as the first weft in the weave of a new fabric. Where that new fabric takes us, we have yet to learn."

AUNT ROSE'S FASHION FACTS

Waycross, Georgia, 1903. It is said that certain people are invisible. But it could also be said that Lydia McAllister was possibly *the* most invisible woman in the history of Waycross, Georgia. A spinster both by choice *and* necessity, she nevertheless carried out her daily duties as though she were indeed visible.

And it was a wonder that no one noticed her, with her odd manner of dress. No matter the weather, she wore a long-sleeved gown with exactly thirty buttons, no more, no less, that ran the length of her bodice. And on her feet, she wore lace-up boots with seventeen holes on one side of each boot and seventeen hooks on the other side. On her hands, she wore white gloves that covered her wrists, and her auburn hair sported a bun covered with a scarf given to her by her aunt Rose. This scarf was by far the most colorful thing about her, the black silk sporting a bouquet of red poppies.

Ever since Rose had died ten years earlier, she had become invisible. When Lydia was out walking people would look up, but as she lifted her hand to wave, they quickly turned away, as though they hadn't seen her. Sometimes she would call a hearty hello only to discover they hadn't heard her either. At first, she merely frowned. Maybe she just hadn't used enough volume, so she would clear her throat and start over.

"Hello there!" she would say in her loudest voice.

But still they walked away as though she were not there, as though she had never spoken, as though she didn't exist. And so, over time, Lydia forgot to say hello, forgot to raise her hand in welcome, forgot to exist except in the narrow confines of her world–her home, her church, her garden.

When standing in front of her bathroom mirror, she would often wonder if the image she saw was really her. If other people looked at that same mirror would they see her? Would they say, "There's Lydia McAllister," or would they simply see themselves? Probably the latter.

At first, it bothered her to no end. *Why can't they see me?* She didn't know. Oh, she knew she wasn't pretty in the strictest sense with her sharp nose and her hooded eyes and her plump lips. But she wasn't ugly either.

When she was younger, she had been an impulsive, curious little girl who would prowl the neighborhood looking for signs of life in this sleepy little town. She would find them too... in the insects and animals. At Kettle Creek, she found pollywogs and salamanders that she would put in big glass bowls until she felt sorry for them. Then she would release them back into the wild. And there was the gray mare down by the railroad tracks. Lydia would pick grass that she found at the roadside and listen to the mare's quiet munching, feel the wet snuffling of lips on her palms as she fed the roan. She would run her hand across the old mare's mane, surprised at how coarse and dusty it felt. Animals were her refuge.

Oh, she knew people had seen her back then, but not in a good way. They would yell, "Get away from that horse. What are you doing by the railroad tracks? Shouldn't you be at home with your parents instead of out galavantin'?"

But she liked galavanting. She liked the railroad tracks. And she especially liked the mare, the pollywogs and salamanders. What she *didn't* like was people always yelling at her, often for no good reason, or at least to her mind. Looking back, Lydia knew that, as a child, she hadn't always thought through the consequences of her actions, but she'd had a good heart.

Now, as an adult, she could almost forget that she was invisible as she walked home from church. Foolishly, she sometimes listened to the warm hellos and reflexively raised a hand and called a greeting only to discover, yet again, that the caller wasn't speaking to her, rather to the person behind her or across the street or seated on a porch swing. Like an inflated balloon with a pinprick, Lydia would quickly deflate, her body sagging in on itself and once again she would be alone in her bubble, walking the streets unknown, unseen. By now she should know not to engage, but a desire to be part of something bigger than herself, to be *known*, would sometimes well up inside her. An elixir best left unexamined. *After all, humans are a social animal, aren't they?*

* * *

Lydia thought her life would continue like this forever. So, it came as a surprise one day when she looked out the window of the Victorian house she had grown up in, the one her parents had left her nearly seven years ago because they'd had no sons or daughters save her. She gazed out over the garden as she sipped on pink lemonade. Already the day was proving to be a hot one. Even the cicadas, which loved heat and chorused its misery, had fallen eerily silent. Her skin pricked.

A presentiment.

And surely, there could be no greater presentiment than when the world fell silent, the insects and animals taking a deep breath. *What could this possibly mean?* After all, if a prowler were afoot, the neighborhood dogs would bay with alarm. No, this was different. It was that tiny hiccup before a tornado, the calm before a torrent of foul weather. And yet, she couldn't quite put her finger on what it was that was bothering her. What the quiet was telling her. And it did speak… in its own way. She had experienced so much silence over a lifetime that she'd learned to listen to the earth's breaths. To the lulls in conversation. What was *not* being said.

Often, the unspoken was more important than what *was* being spoken. She wondered if other people were aware of the lulls, the hints of nature, the interludes in music, drama, comedy… even speech. They were the grace notes, the great portenters. They revealed so much. Provided the "ahas!" in life that most people overlooked.

Lydia peered at the plaque hanging on the wall next to the window that looked out over the backyard. It had been left to her by her aunt who had lived with her as a child. It read: *Genius is not of the conscious, but of the subconscious.*

As Lydia well knew, people constantly filled up their days with noise, drowning out the subconscious and burying it like they had her aunt, in dirt six-feet deep. She sighed as she stared out at the garden.

"I miss her," she said, surprised to hear her voice, surprised that she could even speak amidst so much silence. For some reason, it made her smile. It meant that she was still alive. Still present. Still visible, if only to herself.

Her aunt Rose had been a tiny but amazing woman with a huge heart–a doctor in a time when doctors were all men. Rose studied, read voraciously, and learned the craft by following both doctors and veterinarians on house calls, whenever they would permit it. Fortunately, Doc Druthers had been a kind, patient man who found her a comfort rather than a bother. And since he tended toward drink, she could help him when he found it difficult to perform his daily functions. And yet Rose was not ordinary, and a world was never kind to those who were different, as Lydia well knew.

No, her aunt had been pecked to death like an unwanted chick by the townspeople who didn't understand her… a young woman who was smart and ambitious. Who believed in herself. Who hadn't wanted to live in the narrow confines of hearth and home. Rose had lived a big life, crusading on behalf of the orphans left abandoned by poverty and domestic unrest, crossing the tracks into the colored part of town. It had taken time, but she had been accepted by many on that side of the tracks, even if she was despised by just as many people on her own side. Yet, a woman like her could never have survived without a few benefactors who fought on her behalf, who saw the good in her, who understood that the fabric of society was better as a whole than in the varying threads that separated it.

But now her aunt was gone, and no one had come forward in the past ten years to champion those less fortunate, not even Lydia, who couldn't be seen at any rate.

How can I possibly make a difference when no one even knows I exist?

She, who had been forced into the shadows as a fallout to the town's anger and resentment toward Rose, as she was only now realizing. And yet, if she were to be honest with herself, she wanted to be seen, wanted to make a difference. Most of all, she wanted to be courageous... like her aunt. Ten years of invisibility was enough.

She wiped her brow, the little droplets of sweat now running down her face in tiny rivulets. *Drip, drip, drip.* They seemed to mark off the seconds, the minutes, and the hours of her life in the splash marks they made on the parquet flooring.

Blink, blink, blink.

She could feel her eyelashes brush against the tops of her cheeks, a reminder that she was still here, still waiting... but for what? For life to begin? For people to see her? Or maybe just to become part of the fabric of the small town that had excluded her so completely.

Blink, blink, blink.

For years Lydia had wondered why she had been so totally and completely shunned. Did it have something to do with her aunt's final days in town before Rose, too, had disappeared? She pursed her lips, her eyes taking in the flowers. Something had happened all those years ago and it lingered, even now, like the wisteria on the sultry air of a hot afternoon.

What had taken place then still held Lydia in its web, binding her tighter and tighter to a microcosm of moments spent in situ as she waited to be eaten or released. Or perhaps she was meant to simply fend for herself until time left her desiccated and alone. She prayed that someday she would discover the truth. Learn what had really happened in that year that Rose had disappeared from Waycross, Georgia. Learn why she had returned only to die, shunned by the townsfolk.

What was that old saying? Ah yes! *The truth shall set you free.* She shivered despite the noonday heat.

Once again, she peered out over her garden, abloom with delphiniums, foxglove and violets. Her eyes rested on her apricot Noisette rose, the belle of most southern aristocrat estates. She hoped she could figure life out before she withered into nothing. Hoped she found love before the bloom fell off *her* rose.

Well, time couldn't stand still forever. She had a house to care for, a yard that needed tending, and another day to get through before she could lie in bed reading about the lives of people far different from her own. Lives that were rich and full. Lives that mattered.

With that, she marched into her house, through the hallway and dining room to the kitchen where she poured herself another glass of pink lemonade. She drank down the cool liquid and felt instant relief from what appeared to be, by all accounts, a very muggy day. Then she took one last drink of her lemonade and set her glass on the counter.

On a whim, she removed her auburn hair from its bun and spent the next fifteen minutes French braiding it. Satisfied with her handiwork, she proceeded to her mudroom where she put on her brown leather gardening boots and her big floppy straw hat and leather gloves. She then wandered to the toolshed, enjoying the smells of rusted metal, dank walls, and old lubricating oil. It reminded her of her father, God rest his soul. He had been a big hulking man with long hairy arms, large hands, and a kind face that had drawn her mother to him. They had met at church as mere teens, him with hair that fell across his face and a shy smile; her with a confidence that Lydia had never inherited, and a singular beauty that Lydia had also not inherited.

No, her mother had been born with a halo that encompassed her in everything she did. The townsfolk had loved her, and perhaps that was another reason they had never really seen Lydia, because her mother took up so much of the oxygen in the room that all eyes were on her and her alone. Lydia was the waif who vied for attention, but visitors would merely pat her head like a dog and say "good girl," then forget about her as quickly as they would a mutt.

And yet she had loved her mother and felt the same desire for attention from her that the townsfolk had. But a woman that ebullient, that ephemeral, had too many irons in the fire, followed too many strands in the web of life to be able to focus her attention on a mere child. Therefore, Lydia had been left to her own devices, had sought her own counsel. Had it not been for Rose, she might have disappeared altogether then as she had now.

Be grateful for the good things in life, Rose had reminded her.

And so Lydia decided to focus on her flowers. With tools in hand, Lydia walked out of the shed and peered out at the waves of heat shimmering off the garden soil. She should have weeded either early in the day or later, near dusk, but she'd had church that morning–Saturday service for the overflow crowd, and she definitely fit into *that* category. Tonight, she planned to make a pie–an apple pie perhaps, or peach, she wasn't sure yet. Then she would take a large helping, lie in bed, and eat it while reading a book. Alongside the bed, she would place her fan so that she could cool off, and she would add a big dollop of French vanilla ice cream to her pie. That should help cool her. Just the thought of it made the idea of weeding during the heat of the day more bearable.

"Here we go," she said to herself, grateful that no one was listening so she wouldn't sound like the crazy old spinster that everyone thought she was, even though she was only twenty-seven. But twenty-seven in a town like Waycross, Georgia, was as near to ancient as a woman could get, whereas men were considered young well into their seventies.

Lydia took a tentative step into her yard, trowel in one hand and a large metal bucket in the other. Her hands and torso were covered so all that was exposed was her face, and *that* was shaded by her large floppy hat.

For the next hour, she quietly set to work digging and prodding out dandelion and broadleaf plantain, carpetweed and dog fennel. Even the occasional jimson weed. Slowly but surely, the flowers that edged the front lawn began to take shape into something spectacular. She eyed her peach, old-fashioned English roses, the very same ones she had entered in the Georgia County Fair. She'd won first place with them back when her aunt Rose was still alive. Next, her gaze wandered to her red-and-white caladium that bordered the lawn and glistened like stained-glass windows. Then there were her lime hydrangeas along with the more traditional pinks and blues. And of course one could not forget the black-eyed Susans or the red bee balm that the hummingbirds so loved.

Lydia became so entranced in the tending of her garden that she hadn't noticed a shadow fall over her until she looked up, hand touching the rim of her straw hat.

"Hello there!" a man called in a voice she didn't recognize.

All she could see was a dark silhouette, the outline of a tall slender man with a satchel. She looked behind her to see who he might be talking to, but to her surprise, she saw no one on either side of her fenced yard. And she felt certain he was facing her. When he repeated his greeting, she pointed to her chest, her eyebrows arched in question.

"Me?" she said, but it came out a mewl.

"Aye, how are you doing this fair day?"

"Why, I'm doing well. And you?" she said, her voice stronger now.

She shaded her eyes with her hands and smiled as she realized Rex Henderson had been the one to greet her. He was the resident hobo and possibly the most educated hobo on earth. She'd heard rumors. Harvard graduate conscripted into the Spanish-American War. Shellshock. Afterward, he'd come home a broken man and had disappeared more completely than Lydia herself into the fabric of Waycross society.

"Glad to hear that."

Then before she knew what he was doing, he bent down and picked up the *Waycross Sentinel*.

"It appears the newspaper boy missed the fence. Here!" he said, tossing the newspaper to her. It landed directly in front of her with a loud plop, next to the stone she'd had engraved with her aunt's name on it. "Might want to read it," he said. "There's a storm a-brewin', mark my words."

"Storm?" She looked up at the clear sky, marred only by the wispiest of clouds. "But it's such a lovely day."

"You're right, it *is* a lovely day. Just be careful," he said mysteriously. Then he winked. Winked! Afterward, he tipped his hat and said, "Good day."

Heeding Rex's warning, Lydia peered down at the newspaper and read the headlines. "Yellow Fever Train Heading Our Way." And beneath the headlines: "Three deaths attributed to yellow fever." More to come.

A memory came to her unheeded that caused her to shiver with anxiety, for it drew her back to Rose's illness and the day Rose had died. The day Lydia had realized that Rose had a secret of some sort. A secret that she had taken to her grave.

Lydia rose on unsteady feet, determined to find out exactly what had happened all those years ago that had pushed her to the edges of society. Had caused her to become invisible. And the only way she could do that was to find out what had happened to her aunt Rose.

2

"Fashion is forever changing. The greatest change occurred following the Victorian age. Women, who had dressed more conservatively before the turn of the twentieth century, found new freedom in dress in the Edwardian Age. Sleeves shortened, necklines plunged, and the Gibson Girl gave way to hair that often flowed down a woman's back. Not exactly a sexual revolution, but a loosening of sorts."

AUNT ROSE'S FASHION FACTS

For Lydia, being seen became her new obsession. She felt certain that to find out what had *truly* happened to her aunt Rose, she would first need to be able to speak with the townsfolk, but she couldn't do that as long as she was invisible. So, later that evening, she forgot all about the pie she had planned to bake, and instead traipsed up into the attic. Once there, she pulled her aunt's trunk from the wall and opened it, swatting away the dust motes that danced in the stifling air of the warm attic. Stacked inside were boxes, smelling musty with age. The first was an old Sears and Roebucks box, pale blue, faded further by the aging of time. She lifted the box out and carefully opened the lid. To her surprise and delight, it held the most breathtaking green dress. It was nothing like her plain cream-colored dresses, all nearly identical. No, this one had ruffles around the bodice, puffy sleeves, and yards of lush green fabric that swooped to the floor. Lydia had seen a picture of Rose in this dress as a young woman, when she'd still engaged the idea of a traditional life, before she'd gone to the Women's Medical College of Pennsylvania to train as an M.D., one of the few places in the nation that educated women to become doctors. Lydia hugged the dress to her chest, viewing it from all sides, then set it back into the trunk.

"It's a bit old-fashioned," she said, enjoying the new sound of her voice. She chewed on her top lip, thinking. If she cut the sleeves, removed some of the ruffles, why, it would look almost modern.

Once again, she snatched up the dress, forgetting about her aunt, for the moment. Then she ran downstairs to her sewing room where her Wheeler & Wilson treadle took up one side of the long narrow room. For the next several hours, despite the sultry heat of the mid-July day, she sewed. When she was through, she held up the dress and stood in front of the floor-length mirror that resided in the corner of the room. Satisfied at her handiwork, she rushed upstairs and hung her refurbished dress in her nearly floor-to-ceiling maple chifforobe.

That night, she barely slept, so excited was she to wear her new dress into town as she sought out people who might remember her aunt. Maybe they would be able to shed some light on what had happened all those years ago. By morning, her eyes were swollen from fatigue but her enthusiasm hadn't waned. She ate a breakfast of poached eggs and a small bowl of oatmeal with dried currants. Then she quickly dressed and marched down the front walk.

No sooner had she opened the gate than she nearly ran into old Doc Renwick, who had retired some years back. He turned a dozen shades of red as he fumbled and fussed at the near catastrophe.

"Excuse me," he said.

Lydia was so pleased that the short man with the bulbous nose had noticed her that she overlooked the fact that she had lived at the same address her entire life and been a patient at his surgery as a child, and yet he still seemed to have no clue who she was.

She introduced herself, amazed at her own audacity. Then she fluttered her eyelashes like a young schoolgirl instead of a soon-to-be spinster at twenty-seven.

"Well, I hope to see you again, Miss Lydia," he said, bowing slightly and lifting his bowler hat to expose a partly balding pate. Then he was gone.

Funny how a person could go an entire life unseen and in black and white. Now, suddenly, it was as if small patches of color had appeared in her life, from the gladiolas that lined her neighbor's yard to the yappy Chesapeake Bay Retriever pacing the fence alongside her as she walked toward town.

She heard a loud "ah-oo-gah" horn and turned in time to see the milliner doff his hat in greeting. *Amazing!* Had she awoken to the world or it to her? She wasn't sure. She watched in wonder as the first Model A she'd ever seen chugged past, releasing a puff of gray smoke with a loud whiz-bang. She clasped her hands together in delight. It was cherry red, with black leather seats, white-wall tires and red spokes. She'd read in the *Waycross Sentinel* that the first two had been sold, but she had never imagined that she would get to see one so soon, if ever.

came time to load and unload the food, the water, and the people they had come to rescue.

"I don't know," Mr. Peabody said, his face ashen against the silvery lights. "We take it as it comes."

Lydia tapped a cadence on the floorboards with her serviceable footwear, watching, waiting. At long last, the train came round the bend. As it moved ever closer, Lydia smelled smoke in the distance, riding the currents northward from the bonfire below. It lit the hillside in a hazy orange silhouette of color that made it seem as though the mountainside was aglow. Lydia prayed the fire would buy them the time required to do what they needed to do and return home. But how long could she hope to keep her pursuers at bay? And who had started the bonfire? Surely not Gladys.

"Be ready," Mr. Peabody said as the train lurched to a stop, the brakes squealing so that the devil himself could hear them should he so choose. The sound reverberated in Lydia's chest.

As though unleashed, Lydia jumped down and together the two began stacking the food next to the train as it moved forward then backward, over and over until the tank car was firmly attached to the rest of the train. Next, the railroad men filled the engine with water. Finally, a porter jumped out of the restaurant car, then another and another. Soon, a whole host of workers exited the train and made quick work of the food storage bins that Lydia and the women had filled with every manner of food from fried chicken to okra with bacon crumbles, cheese grits, and even black-eyed peas.

With something akin to panic now, Lydia watched as the first family tentatively alighted from a car near the back, a black family... Jewel's family.

"What do we do?" Lydia hissed. "Jewel and her husband aren't here yet."

"We cross that bridge when we come to it," Mr. Peabody said, urging Lydia forward as he went to help the family with their meager belongings.

Lydia followed suit, leading a woman that could only be Jewel's sister-in-law, a thin, willowy woman, her hair done in a twist that framed her narrow features. The woman grabbed hold of her daughter's hand, while the man at her side held a frightened young boy in his arms.

"This way," Lydia urged.

"Where is Jewel?" the woman asked, clearly as frightened as her young son.

"She's not here yet."

The woman stopped, fear making her voice rise as she said, "She's not here?"

"Keep moving," Lydia hissed. "She should be here any moment." And although she hoped that was true, she couldn't be sure. Still, they needed to do *something*.

Once they had the family situated next to the cart, they went in search of Mr. Peabody's relatives, this time sprinting toward the front of the train, where the white passengers were located. After several minutes of moving back and forth between cars, they finally saw the family rushing toward the exit, bags in hand.

"Hurry!" Mr. Peabody urged, helping them down off the train and running with them across the tracks and onto the dirt road beyond where the cart lay waiting.

"Now what?" Lydia asked. Time was running out. The bonfire, which had only minutes ago lit the night sky, was starting to die back. Without the fire to block their exit, if indeed that was part of the diversion, the vigilantes would soon be headed this way. They couldn't wait for Jewel and her husband forever.

"I'm afraid there's been a change of plans," Mr. Peabody said to the two families. "I'll load you all in the back of the truck."

"What then?" asked Jewel's brother in a deep voice. Although much larger than Jewel, he bore her clear skin and large, almond-shaped eyes.

"I don't know," Mr. Peabody said, his shoulders slumped.

They all looked at each other with resignation, then apparently deciding they had no other options, the two families walked around to the back of the cart as Mr. Peabody loaded them and their baggage inside the cold damp interior. The slam of the door behind them resounded in Lydia's chest, and she felt a wave of emotion wash over her at the unknown future that lay ahead for each of them.

Lydia and Mr. Peabody lingered for no more than a second before taking their stations inside the cab, Mr. Peabody in the driver's seat and Lydia in the passenger seat. Reluctantly, Mr. Peabody whipped at the reins and gave a feeble "hah" as the horses clomped into action, turning abruptly toward the direction they'd come.

For the next five minutes, the pair sat next to each other in silence, each lost in their own thoughts. Lydia had nearly given up on the idea that they could come away from this unscathed when, to her immense relief, she saw Jewel waving a hand from a small carriage coming toward them. Fortunately, this was not one of the Vigilance Committee or their ilk, but rather the salvation of the two families. Lydia had barely got the words "there's Jewel and her husband" out of her mouth when Mr. Peabody shouted, "Hallelujah!"

Moments later, the small black four-seater carriage pulled up beside them. Inside were Jewel and her husband George. He was a big, strapping man. She wondered where they had found the beautiful carriage as few could afford such a luxury, but didn't ask. Better not to know. She did notice that the left side carriage lamp was broken. Whoever the carriage belonged to would want it back before the night was through, no doubt.

They all exited their vehicles, Mr. Peabody opening up the rear door of the cart and helping the others out. They said their quick "how-d'ya-dos" and then fell into silence, each wrapped in their own thoughts, each with their own worries.

"We had trouble with transportation," Jewel said by way of explanation, then left it at that.

Lydia felt as though all of the air had been drained from her lungs and her head swam with lack of oxygen. After brief hugs and handshakes, the two families forged their way into the small vehicle, husbands on the seats, wives on their laps, and the two children squeezed between the pair, while one child sat on Jewel's lap up front.

They were about to leave when Mr. Peabody leaned in and handed his family a wad of bills. Lydia did the same with the other family. "For food, and anything else they might need," Mr. Peabody said.

They broached no argument. The weary passengers merely offered their thanks and then were on their way.

When they were gone, Mr. Peabody shouted, "Hurry and get in, Miss Lydia."

Once inside and moving, Lydia said, "Thanks for everything, Mr. Peabody."

"Call me Charles, though most call me Chip. After tonight, I think we're on a first name basis, don't you?"

"Mr... Charles, I mean Chip," she said, grateful for everything he had done to help the two families tonight... *and* the people on the train.

He reached around and grabbed a couple of Royal Crown Colas he'd kept behind the seat for just this occasion, she felt certain, and handed her one.

"There's a bottle opener in the driver's box," he said, nodding his head toward the wooden box at her feet.

After a brief struggle with the lid, she lifted it and indeed found a bottle opener. She opened his first, then hers. Together they drank in silence. By the time they reached the twist in the road that would take them back to the railroad tracks, the fire in the distance had died down even further. Though far away, sounds carried in the night and she could hear pops and dull shouts, as though the earlier melee had turned into an all-out brawl. Silently, she prayed that Gladys was all right and would arrive back safely.

"Uh-oh," she said as the fire winked out completely. Whatever had kept the men contained now burst like a dam, for an eerie glow of headlights flowed out in a wide arc as the carriages raced out of town toward the main entrance to the switchyard. "How long have we got?"

"Ten minutes tops before they're on this side of the tracks. Hold on tight. I know a place where we can hide until they pass, but it's anyone's guess who will make it there first."

She had scarcely heeded his words and grabbed onto the side of the buckboard before the whip cracked against first one, then the other horse's back. The animals reared up into the air before taking off at a speed that rattled Lydia's teeth together and thrust her side to side, her hip hitting the wooden railing. If not for her quick reflexes she might have been thrown to the ground and run over by the cart. As it were, she fought for air as the cart twisted one way then the next, wheels rising up off the ground as if to topple or take flight.

In slow motion, she saw the carriage lamps in the horse-drawn carriages move as if segments of a caterpillar, lit from within, while Mr. Peabody had purposely kept their lamp unlit so as not to be observed.

Hurry. Hurry. Hurry. She willed the horses on, wishing they could read her thoughts and magically carry out her wishes.

The string of lights now appeared at the train tracks. Soon, the marauders would be upon them and all would be lost. Lydia closed her eyes and whispered a silent prayer. Just as she opened them, the carriage bolted to the right and the horses jolted to a hasty halt inside a turnout in a deep copse, narrowly avoiding a spill. For several seconds, the cart shuddered and the horses tossed their heads from side to side in protest.

Despite his age, the agile Mr. Peabody leaped from the buckboard onto the back of the horse on the left, leaning in and murmuring comforting sounds into the horse's ear. When it had sufficiently calmed, he leaped to the ground and grabbed each horse by the bit, murmuring more encouraging words that held an undertone of menace should the horses refuse to maintain calm. Fortunately for them both, the horses heeded the man's warnings and quieted just enough to keep them from rearing up when the sounds of carriages and riders whizzed past, one after another in an almost endless procession. It seemed an eternity before the sounds of hooves and wheels against the rutted dirt road had subsided and they could proceed.

The trip back seemed to take much less time than the trip there, and to Lydia's immense relief, Mr. Peabody let her out close to her house, but at a far enough distance and quiet enough location that hopefully none would be the wiser. They said brief goodbyes. Lydia didn't know how she could ever thank the man, nor he her, by the moistness she saw in his eyes. She knew they weren't out of the woods yet, but at least she would feel safe, once she made it home.

For the next ten minutes she raced across town, hoping to put distance between her and the men in their carriages. Scarcely had she reached the alleyway in sight of her house when she tripped over a root wad and fell to the ground. Her knees were skinned and bloody, the wind knocked out of her. It took several minutes to recover. She attempted to lift herself up when, out of the darkness, she felt a warm hand and smelled motor oil and grease. And something else. Sulfur, perhaps.

"You okay, Miss?" the man said, helping her to her feet.

Lydia jerked away in fear, hoping against hope that he wasn't from the Vigilance Committee. Instead, she peered up with apprehension into the eyes of the town hobo who wandered the backroads and spent his nights next to trash cans in search of a spare meal, or under the cover of a makeshift shelter.

Rex Henderson. The hobo who had warned her of a storm brewing. One of the Henderson boys–before the Spanish American War had turned the sweet, mild-mannered young man into a hardened soldier. Five years of suffering the aftereffects of the war–shell shocked, she had heard it called–had led him to this. A life on the streets. It saddened her to think of it.

The irony was, he had been the first to truly see her. In some small way, by acknowledging her that day in her garden, he had helped make her visible again, and for that, she would be forever grateful. She smiled at the memory then turned her thoughts once again to Rex.

He had to be in his thirties, near as she could tell, and harmless by all accounts. Everyone loved him. He was a fixture of the community, an apparition that hid in the shadows, that encompassed all the ills of the town as though, like Jesus, he had taken on the sins and bore them as his own personal cross. She dusted off her hands and thanked him. She was about to turn and leave when she stopped.

"Would you like to come inside... for a bath and a hot meal?"

Ordinarily, as a single woman, she wouldn't have asked a man into her home, though it was common enough for families to invite hobos in for a meal in most Southern homes. But this was not an ordinary night and these were not ordinary circumstances. Besides, she knew his family and liked them immensely.

"I wouldn't want to impose," he said in a deep voice that spoke of cigarettes and cheap wine.

"Actually, I could use the company."

"You're sure... no one will talk?" He, like she, knew what a small town could do when they got hold of a tidbit of gossip and worried it like a bone.

"It's dark out. I think it will be okay."

Despite the inky blackness of the night, she knew his eyes were blue and his skin tanned from days spent in the sun.

"Thanks, ma'am." She heard the unmistakable gratitude in his voice.

"Come on, you can meet Webster."

"Webster?"

"My dog."

"Webster," he said, rolling the name around on his tongue.

As they neared the low white fence that led to her backyard, she peered toward the garage, the silence deafening. *Please let the motor car be there and Gladys safe.* With trepidation, she entered the yard and quickly checked in the garage. Her heart lodged in her throat when she discovered that her new motor car was still missing and with it, Gladys. She could do nothing about it now except pray, which she had been doing plenty of throughout the night.

For the next several hours, as Rex washed up, she set about heating water on the stove for the bath, while she rewarmed some of the leftovers from the meals they had prepared the other day.

Just as she was finished setting the plates and food on the

table, Rex entered the kitchen and pulled out a chair to sit, his wet hair combed neatly to the side. Clean and smelling better, he nodded his thanks. He now wore a pair of overalls and a shirt she'd found of her father's, the hunger apparent in the lean set of his jaw. Once at the table, he ate and ate for so long that she thought he might burst. By the time he stood, his bloodshot eyes drooped and his steps were slow, his back bent with fatigue.

"Why don't I make up a bed in the spare room?" she asked.

"I couldn't put you out like that, Miss Lydia."

"It's no problem, Mr. Henderson."

Rex stopped, his eyes moist at her use of the title. No doubt he was used to being called any number of names, but it had left an impression that she had used his last name.

"Now," she said, before he could wax nostalgic, "let's find you a quilt and a pillow."

She ushered him to the spare bedroom, then sat out on the back porch waiting for Gladys to return. Lydia struggled over the idea of whether she should go into town to search for Gladys and risk possible exposure for either herself or her friend. Knowing Gladys, she might very well have returned home by now and was, at this moment, getting her three winks while Lydia sat up half the night worried about her. No matter. If she didn't hear from her by morning, she would go in search of her friend, risk or no risk.

Midway through the night, Lydia brought out an old army blanket of her father's and covered herself in it as she lay down on the wooden bench swing. Her last words, before she drifted off into a deep slumber that lifted only at dawn, were *Please, God, keep Gladys safe.*

9

From the Archives of Joan Elaine Fields, M.D.:

"It is said that clothes make a man or a woman. They reveal character, station within society, even happiness or sadness. Mourning clothes let us know that a person is grieving. Whereas a white lace wedding dress with ribbons and flowers can reveal an eagerness to begin a new life, to participate in society's many functions—a hopefulness, as it were."

AUNT ROSE'S FASHION FACTS

To Lydia's surprise, she awoke on the back porch to the smell of frying bacon and coffee. It took her a moment to gather herself, the memory of last night returning as she took stock of the fact that she had slept the entire night on the porch and had yet to hear from Gladys. For one brief second, she had forgotten about Mr. Henderson or that she had invited him to spend the night. He must be in the kitchen preparing breakfast.

At the smell of bacon, her stomach rumbled as though only now realizing that she had forgotten to eat last night, she'd been so worried about Gladys. Before she went to see about breakfast, she ran out to the tool shed and threw the doors open, her body sagging when she saw that it was still empty.

Where are you, Gladys?

Her mind entertained any number of scenarios, bouncing back and forth between hope that Gladys had merely decided to drive the new motor car to her house, due to the lateness of the hour, and fear that her new friend had been attacked and was even now in the hospital or dead.

No, I refuse to go there.

It would do no good for her to fear the worst. She quickly closed the garage and walked back to her two-story Victorian, its white gables tossing shadows in the early morning light. Once inside the foyer that connected to the kitchen, she shivered, whether from the coolness of the morning or the lingering, pernicious fear, she couldn't say. She only knew that her stomach continued to rumble from deep within her belly at the aroma emanating from the kitchen.

"Mornin', ma'am," Rex said, nodding slightly.

Cleaned up, he looked like a new man. She had even offered him her father's old razor and a pair of scissors so that he could shave and trim his hair. The only thing that prevented him from appearing like any other town's member was his clothing. No doubt realizing that he would be leaving today, he had changed out of her father's clothing and had dressed in his street clothes which, even at this distance, reeked of stale cigarettes and grime. She could wash them, or...

"Mr. Henderson, could I interest you in some of my father's old clothes? To take with you, I mean. You're about the same size as he was. Anything that doesn't fit, I could hem up or sew to suit you. What do you say?" she said with such a cheery spin that he could hardly say no.

He must have realized it too, because he gave a short chuckle and threw up his hands, spatula and all.

"Let me have you sort through his clothes," she said, "then I can finish up here."

With that, they left the meal to simmer while she took him upstairs, opening the armoire and the chifferobe in her parents' room, which she'd left pretty much as it had been before they died. Both her parents had come down with influenza during the big 1890 pandemic, and although they hadn't died then, their lungs had become so weakened that when another, less virulent bout came around, they succumbed within a short time of each other. Yet, she couldn't help but wonder if they'd died of a broken heart when the town shunned them because of "Rose and her antics," as one particularly loathsome woman from church had put it. Sadly, Lydia laid out her father's shirts, pants, coats, socks, and even shoes for Mr. Henderson to sort through. Seeing them, she felt a sharp pang in her chest, feeling the loss as though it were fresh.

"Take anything you like–or all of them, for that matter."

"I wouldn't have anywhere to keep more than a couple changes of clothing," he said, fingering the clothing longingly.

"Oh," she said, realizing she hadn't thought through the complications he might face with a life on the road. "Well, all the same, take a look, try them on. Anything you want, you can have… and I can save back what you can't take with you for later," she added as an afterthought. "Just set aside anything you want and I will package it up for you."

Rex thanked her. She was touched by the deep kindness of his eyes despite the inequities that life had dealt him. For one brief moment, she felt like crying. But that wouldn't do, she decided, so she turned on her heels and hurried downstairs to finish up the breakfast.

"Miss McAllister." He nodded perfunctorily. "We've received some most unsavory news."

"Oh?" she said, praying that her voice didn't tremble.

"Is it true that you had a rendezvous with those folks from the train on the night of the bonfire?"

She breathed deeply to steady herself, then said, "It is." Hopefully, they believed it was her at the train station instead of Gladys. Had they known she was on the other side of the tracks, no telling what they would do.

"After all that we spoke about the other day, knowing full well that you were bringing disease to our community?"

"How so?" she asked.

His cheeks puffed up and he blinked rapidly, clearly surprised that she had the audacity to be so bold.

"Why, surely you've heard about Mortimer and Claudia Shipke."

The air suddenly felt claustrophobic. "Claudia is sick now too?" she asked, aghast at this latest news.

"Why, yes," he said, his dark brows hooding his eyes. "You have single-handedly brought yellow fever into our community. What do you have to say for yourself?"

The entire crowd erupted at that until the Mayor had to turn around, put two fingers in his mouth and whistle as loudly as he could. "Silence!" he shouted in case there was a soul within a half-mile distance who hadn't heard the whistle.

Slowly, the crowd quieted.

"Now, explain yourself," he said with a nod to Lydia.

"First of all, from what I've heard, Mr. Shipke came down with yellow fever *before* the train ever stopped," Lydia said, noting the murmur that rose like flies around those gathered. "Secondly, even if they *had* come down with it after the train stopped, neither Claudia *nor* her husband Mort was around the train or anyone on it, so how could they have caught the fever from them?"

To her relief, she saw a few nodding heads, and the murmur of discontent at least seemed mixed now. She even heard a few clamor to add, "Yes, answer *that* Mayor Thornesby." A roll of thunder stretched out like the hand of God himself reaching down to shake all those present. People looked to the sky for lightning, the flashes coming closer now.

"What about them Nigras you helped?" Dottie's husband, Bedford, shouted from somewhere in the crowd. Lydia searched until she saw the stout little man who had obviously enjoyed Dottie's cooking because he was nearly as wide as Dottie only with the addition of a pot belly. "A family over there came down sick as a direct result of you helping people off that train."

He knows.

Lydia felt a chill run through her. And as if to further that feeling, a clap of thunder pealed overhead, followed by another flash of lightning moments later. And yet, weather aside, she refused to roll over and play dead, even for Dottie's husband, despite the fact that she, like everyone else in Waycross, adored the effervescent Dottie and both feared and loathed her husband.

"First, there's a good chance those across the tracks had it *well* before the train arrived. Secondly, they live far from any neighbors and have no transportation, for that matter. Like Mort and Claudia, they too have been nowhere near anyone on the train. Yellow fever is rampant throughout many places in the South this summer. If we spent as much time trying to find out what causes it as we do turning on each other, we might actually come up with a solution that could help *us all*."

Before she or anyone else could respond, another clap of thunder sounded, followed by pouring rain that came down in sheets. Wave upon wave sent people clamoring for cover. Within minutes, the crowd had begun to disperse.

"You haven't heard the last of this, Miss Lydia," Mayor Thornesby said, his nose now as red as his jowls and his eyes appearing soulful yet with the slightest tinge of malice. And yet, beneath it all, Lydia couldn't help but think that part of this was bluster on behalf of Bedford. The mayor's eyes were too wide, and they kept darting to the side as though to inform her that he was being coerced by those on the Committee. "You take care to mind your own business in the future, or the Vigilance Committee will come calling."

Lydia didn't have the fight left in her to ask what he meant by "come calling." She could only imagine. For now, she was just grateful to be able to put this horrible episode behind her, even if for only a while.

Wet now from the gales of wind and rain that shot under the eave of the porch, blistering her with tiny pellets of hail that had begun falling, Lydia rushed inside. Rex had been watching from the window, clearly unwilling to become involved in her troubles. Thankfully, she understood why. At least with women, there was some saving grace, but with men there was none. She understood that about her community and it galled her the trouble she might have caused Rex.

"Here," Rex said, "why don't you get dried off, and I'll go fetch us some tea." Webster barked. "Don't worry. I haven't forgotten you." He winked.

The two set off in the lead while Lydia went through the kitchen and upstairs to her room at the back of the house to change out of her wet clothes, all the while pondering what the mayor had said. She couldn't help but wonder what would happen next. Sometimes truth wasn't enough in a small town. And rules came before decency. When that happened, a town could be volatile. Lightning might just be the prelude to something worse. Even in the best of times, summer heat could act as a tinderbox. One match could ignite a fire, and with the right wind, a fire could spread. She just hoped the rain had been enough to put a damper on the anger that seemed to be simmering throughout the community.

Then Lydia thought of her aunt Rose. Of the firestorm that had ignited *her* summer and that of the townspeople so many years ago. Eventually, cooler heads had prevailed. But not before it had taken its toll on everyone around both Lydia and her family, but especially her aunt Rose.

18

From the Archives of Joan Elaine Fields, M.D.:

"It seems I have angered some people in this town and have been told I am no longer welcome to write articles for The Sentinel. *So be it. Still, I hope that you will all take the opportunity to stand before a mirror this morning and take a look at yourselves. So many here consider themselves good Christians, and yet in times of trial, instead of helping each other, we turn on one another.*

"As Christians, we are told to show brotherly love, and yet how often do we turn a blind eye to those in need? 'Get a job,' you say, and yet you refuse to give people jobs because they are not of the same class as you, or the same color, or for any number of foolish reasons.

"The Industrial Revolution has created a huge shift in today's labor market. It has changed our society from an agrarian economy to a wage-based economy where more people are working in factories than on farms. Women are left alone to manage households, while men and children are sent off to work, often in appalling conditions. Lack of time together and fatigue have eroded the traditional family, making it less cohesive.

"In my last column, I used fashion as a metaphor to suggest that maybe it's time to live a little. To remember to be our best selves, to have fun, to love each other. Let us not forget that we have shared, in varying measure, in the back-breaking labor of industry. So, doesn't it seem only fair that we share in the fruits of that labor?"

AUNT ROSE'S FASHION FAUX PAS,
NEW CIRCULAR FOUNDED BY ROSE WATSON AFTER HER OUSTER
FROM THE WAYCROSS SENTINEL

Lydia closed the medical book she had found on one of the bookshelves in the library but kept the faded editorial piece. So many memories came rushing back of that awful day that had led to the entire family being ostracized. Funny how she had blocked it from her memory. The response to Rose's editorial had been swift and punishing. If not for those who had loved and supported her over the course of her lifetime, she might never have survived the backlash.

If only Lydia had read this article *before* she had sewn herself back into the fabric of the community, then she might have been able to spare herself the trial that *she* was now facing with the townsfolk. She might have remained hidden away in the rambling Victorian house that had belonged to her family–a mere shadow of a human being–but at least she would have been safe. Lived in at least marginal comfort.

Well, she couldn't change history, either hers *or* Rose's. She simply had to ride this current wave of unrest and hope she survived.

She set the book aside in the musty attic and decided to get busy. Like one of the snapping turtles from the Okefenokee Swamp, it would be easy to disappear into her shell and pretend that yesterday's gathering on her lawn hadn't happened, but it had. And she feared this was only the first volley. She knew she couldn't hide any longer. If people thought they could intimidate her, they would, and what kind of life would she have then? None. And she wasn't going to stop helping people. There was simply too much need.

Just then, Webster entered the room. "So, what do *you* think?" she said, scratching him behind his ears.

He just looked at her, tail swiping at the dust motes on the floor.

She trudged downstairs, Webster passing her and waiting for her at the bottom of the landing. Next, she went in search of Rex. She'd asked him to move the etched stone she'd dedicated to her aunt Rose from the front yard, where Rex had first given her the newspaper and told her about the storm brewing. Now they would be spending more time in the backyard, and she wanted to be able to see it when she was working or enjoying the outdoors. And there the stone sat. Rex, bless his heart, had planted a pink "old garden" rose next to it, its lineage traced back to China, along with a myriad of other low-growing flowers that added color to the mix.

She peered across the wide expanse of lawn to see Rex tending her vegetable garden in overalls, a blue plaid shirt and a wide straw hat. It gave her an idea. She rushed back to her utility room and returned with a large willow basket, which she set beside the zucchini spilling over the edge of the garden onto the lawn.

Kneeling down on a quilted pad that she had made for just this purpose, she began plucking zucchini while Rex weeded.

Without preamble, he said, "You're going back there?" He stared straight ahead, refusing to look at her.

"I have to," she said, moving on to the green beans. "Do you think I'm being foolish?"

"No. You have to show people you're not afraid." Rex used a two-pronged tool to pull up the cheatgrass, an especially virulent weed that could take over a lawn if not kept in check. He placed a clump of it into a metal bucket to dispose of later.

"That's what I thought."

"You'll have enough vegetables for your pantry then?" he said, eying the basket.

Lydia laughed at the idea. "One thing my daddy taught me is to always grow more food than you need. That way when times are hard, you have something to share with the neighbors."

For the next half hour, they worked in silence, talking only sporadically as Rex quit what he was doing to come help her. Together they picked tomatoes, onions, okra, corn, potatoes, a watermelon, turnip greens, collard greens, a few casaba melons and last but not least, cucumbers. They had picked so many vegetables that Rex had gone for a second large harvesting basket with a porcelain handle.

Once the two baskets were filled and both types of melons placed in a wooden crate and put into the Model A's trunk, they set about culling potted meats from the shelves of the cool basement.

"This fall, I'll go hunting and help you preserve more meat," Rex offered, "if you don't think you'll have enough to get you through winter."

"Thanks. I may take you up on that," she said.

For the next ten minutes, they gathered canning jars filled with pears, cherries, apples and other assorted fruits or vegetables so that when the fresh food was gone the Freeman family would have something to eat.

"You know the church has probably helped the family by now," he said, stating the obvious.

"I hope so," she said, "but better to be sure. I won't see those children starve."

She said it with such conviction that Rex threw up his hands and took a step back, as if to ward off any further protest on her part.

"Sorry," she said as she set a final jar of peaches into the wooden box she had placed on the floor. "I didn't mean to get on my high horse."

Rex dipped his head, his hair hiding his face, but not before she'd seen a grin. So, he wasn't opposed to women with a strong mind. Thank heavens! After all, it was too late to put the genie back in the bottle on *that* count.

When they were through, they closed up the house and prepared for the ride into the country. Lydia started to climb into the passenger seat, but Rex stopped her with a hand on the door.

"It's time you learned how to drive, Miss Lydia."

For several seconds, they just stood there staring at each other. Finally, knees quaking, Lydia said, "Are you sure?"

"I'm sure. If I could learn to drive in just a few hours of practice and no training, you can learn." He favored her with a devilish grin. "Besides, let's give those old biddies something to *really* talk about, eh?" He held out his arm and walked her to the driver's side of the vehicle. "M'lady?"

He offered her his hand so that she could step up onto the running board into the driver's seat. It gave her a thrill as she sat behind the steering wheel, a voile veil tied to her straw hat to keep it from flying away.

"What do I do?" she asked, nerves causing her hands to tingle, any previous training by the Ford representative now out the window.

"Watch me." He cranked the engine which started up with a sputter. The entire automobile rumbled beneath her with a loud roar as though ready to take off with or without her.

"Okay," he said, hopping in next to her, "push down on the clutch with your foot."

"Remind me... what's a clutch?"

He pointed at her left foot and the clutch pedal on the floor.

"Now what?" she asked, her hands trembling.

"Push the pedal to the floor."

"Next?"

"While the clutch is on the floor, put the transmission into reverse."

She raised a brow.

"Grab the gear shift knob like this," he said, showing her where to put her hand. "Now slowly let the clutch up while pressing on the gas pedal with your right foot," he added, heading her off at the pass.

The car sputtered a few times, then died. Rex got out of the motor car and cranked the engine once again. After three attempts, she finally got the hang of it and was able to back out of the garage, careful to exit without hitting anything. By the time the vehicle came to a rest in the alleyway, she was panting and out of breath.

"Okay, now you put it into gear and circle around," he said, helping her turn the wheel as she circumnavigated the cul de sac. "See, you're an old pro."

She laughed at that. "If I'm a pro, then watch out world!"

They were in high spirits by the time she reached the road that would take her over the tracks and into the other side of town. And even finer spirits still once she was out in the country heading for the Okefenokee Swamp.

The swamp had always held a certain fascination and mystery in her mind where alligators, cottonmouths, coral snakes, and copperheads weren't the only deadly creatures. The swamp held giant fishing spiders and snapping turtles. Even some of the plants, like the Venus flytrap and the pitcher plants, were carnivorous, either sucking their tiny unsuspecting victims into a round maw filled with acids or working like traps used to capture insects with teeth that allowed only the smallest to escape, the plant devouring the rest.

Now that Lydia felt more comfortable driving, she began wiping the sweat from her neck and brow with a handkerchief she had rolled up in her sleeve.

"It sure has been a humid summer! We've had more rain than I can ever recall." She glanced over at Rex who wore his straw hat low over his eyes to keep the sun from baking him further, his skin already a deep chestnut from the intermittent sun.

As they neared their destination, Rex began swatting at mosquitoes that thickened the closer they got to the water—another hazard of the swamps.

"Why aren't the mosquitoes bothering you?" he asked.

"This," she said, reaching into her small handbag and bringing up a brown vial of liquid.

He held it up to the light and swished it from side to side. "What is it?"

"Citronella oil mixed with jojoba oil to keep it from irritating the skin. You put it on your skin and it keeps mosquitoes and ticks away."

"Aw," he said, shaking the bottle. "Is that why you smell like lemons, Miss Lydia? I thought you were wearing perfume."

"Try it." When he made a face she said, "Better than getting bit. When I was a girl, my parents brought me out here for a picnic. I counted twenty-three mosquito bites on a single leg."

That was the clincher. He sat up and began dousing himself with it.

"Hey, go easy, Mr. Henderson. A little goes a long way."

A blush of crimson crept up his neck and into his face, his

smile reminding her of a schoolboy who had been caught looking at the class grades before they had been posted. She smiled and patted his hand.

"Use as much as you like."

For some reason, that only flustered him further. Fortunately, they had arrived onto the deeply rutted road that led to the Freemans' shack. As if lying in wait, all eight kids came running out onto the porch appearing much healthier than they had the last time she'd seen them, each child having filled out in the week that she'd been away. A wave of relief flooded through her at the sight.

The children swarmed around the vehicle until she thought she might run into one should she fail to put on the brake, which she pressed down immediately. Then, as though they had been saving their words just for her, they all began speaking at once, each clamoring to be heard over the other.

The group divided in two, one group circling Rex as he stepped out of the vehicle, while the other did the same with her as she attempted to steady her feet on the baked mud that edged the farthest reaches of the swamp.

"Hey, Miss Lydia!" Jedediah called, all smiles, this time around.

A girl, who couldn't have been much more than eight, her dress torn and coated in splotches of dirt and mud, came forward and introduced herself as Pearl. "Mama and Daddy are lookin' a mite better," she said shyly. "Jewel come around and treated Mama and Daddy with some garlic and feverwort."

Lydia didn't know that garlic would help, but it certainly hadn't hurt, by the looks of things because there, on the porch, stood Marybeth, the mother of the eight children. And although she didn't appear hale and hearty, by any means, she was standing and that was a start.

"How is Joe, Miss Freeman?" Lydia asked after saying a brief hello and introducing herself again in case the woman had been too ill to recall their former meeting.

"Come see for yo'self, Miss Lydia," Marybeth answered, ushering her inside. "Jewel told us what you did for us."

"I would hope the same would be done for me," Lydia said, embarrassed by the thanks.

"How come you ain't afraid to come out here, Miss Lydia?" Marybeth asked, peering one last time through the open screen door as if one of the swamp creatures were on her porch.

"Who said I wasn't afraid?" Lydia attempted a wan smile.

Marybeth worried her hands, the unspoken question lying between them: Had the Vigilance Committee intimidated Lydia? Truth was, Lydia *had* felt intimidated when Bedford and the others had shown up on her lawn. If only they understood that she wasn't trying to stir anything up. She was just trying to help people in need–people who had been too long ignored. People who were living on the edge.

"Well, I thank you for comin', Miss Lydia," Marybeth said, offering her a cup of coffee, chicory by the smell of it. "I wish I could offer you some lemonade on this warm day, but we don't have a cooler."

"That's okay," Lydia said, mopping her brow. She knew the Freemans couldn't afford to have ice delivered so far from the city, if ever. As such, they had no ice box.

Fortunately, Rex came to the rescue. "I packed a thermos full of ice cold lemonade before we left, Miss Lydia. I think there's enough for all of us."

While he went to retrieve the gallon-sized thermos, Lydia turned back to Marybeth, grateful that Rex had thought ahead.

"How are you getting along with supplies?" Lydia asked.

"Our townsfolk have been real kind to us, Miss Lydia."

To prove it, she brought Lydia around to a large cabinet that sat on the screened porch out back. She opened it to reveal row upon row of canned goods, each facing proudly outward–peas, corn, condensed sweet milk, kippered herrings, potted meat, peaches, pears and a number of other goods.

"What we could *really* use is some fresh fixin's. Our chiles' gums are bleedin'. Sign a mal-nu-trition, Jewel says."

Rex had told Lydia that Marybeth had only a third-grade education before she'd been forced to stay home and work on her family's farm–unlike Jewel, who was highly educated and would have gone far had she been born to white parents. And that was the rub. Intelligence didn't matter. If you were born a woman or of a color deemed unacceptable to society–or were different in any way, for that matter–your opportunities were far fewer. But then again, rising to the top was no picnic either, Lydia realized. Someone was always there to knock you off your pedestal. Truth is, life was hard, more so for some than for others.

At that moment, Rex arrived with the lemonade. Like in *The Pied Piper*, the eight kids followed him in, clamoring with excitement, each talking at once. When Lydia reentered the kitchen, Rex was already pulling down cups from a cupboard kept hidden only by a feed sack.

Each time Rex opened the spigot, a chorus of "Me firsts" arose like the tinkling notes of a choir. "Adults first," Rex said, reminding them of their manners. Once the adults present had been cared for, he handed out drinks, youngest first. The din didn't subside until the eldest, Jedidiah, had a drink in hand.

"Mind if I look in on Joe, take him a lemonade?" Rex asked politely.

"I would like to check on him, too, if you don't mind, Mrs. Freeman," Lydia added.

Marybeth seemed tickled to have been called by her formal

name, her wan face breaking into a smile that reminded Lydia of what she might have looked like had the years and summers spent toiling on a hot farm been kinder to her.

In the dark recesses of the room, little more than a clapboard lean-to attached to the main house, the shriveled little man was now sitting up, aided by a pillow. He appeared less wizened and... dare she say it, healthier. Relief flooded her at the thought that the locals had come together to save these two lives, and eight others, for that matter.

She spent the next twenty minutes visiting the pair. Then she and Rex brought in crates and baskets of fresh fruit and vegetables, which created another stir, louder than the first, if at all possible.

After they had said their goodbyes and were headed back home, Lydia and Rex pulled over into an open glen and sat in the vehicle snacking on cold meat sandwiches that they had made for themselves, along with pickles and an apple each. Close to home now, they finished off their picnic with a small portion of the water meant for the Model A, should it overheat, which it was apt to do on a long journey. Reluctantly, they packed up and set about for the final trek home.

They had just crossed Main Street when Lydia spotted one of the newspaper urchins in brown pants and jacket hawking the *Waycross Sentinel* from a dusty corner, shouting "Paper for sale, paper for sale, get your paper here," in a rhythmic chant. She was about to proceed east toward home when she felt an inexplicable pull, that thing that could only be described as women's intuition. She steered her car close to the boy, ignoring the ringing bells of the carriages and the shouts.

"Five cents a copy," the newsboy yelled. "Get your copy here!"

Lydia dug into her purse and brought out a five-cent piece. She thanked the boy, then glanced at the paper. Her heart nearly stopped as she saw her face splashed on the front page. The headline read: "Lydia McAllister Brings Yellow Fever to Waycross, Georgia."

19

From the Archives of Joan Elaine Fields, M.D.:

"After tobacco and sugar, cotton was considered one of the true luxuries of the 19th and 20th centuries. Cotton gins fed the textile revolution and with it a revolution in fashion—cotton and tulle with crochet, lace, and beautiful braid work now all the rage.

"But this revolution had its roots in a much darker place. A trade in slavery that valued slaves in America as a commodity rather than as a group of individuals. Prior to The Civil War, the value of their labor equaled seven times the currency in circulation at that time. For this reason, a form of slavery followed Reconstruction called the Black Codes, whereupon Negroes were forced to sign yearly labor contracts or risk arrest or reentry into the system of unpaid labor. These relics of the war continued well into the 19th century, its lingering effects still evident today."

AUNT ROSE'S FASHION FAUX PAS

"I cannot believe that once again Rose Watkins is creating a stir in our town by questioning the plantation system that has offered work, food,

Lydia recounted the headline of the newspaper to Rex as she drove headlong down Main Street in her cherry red motor car.

"Can you believe it? The writer accused me of having brought yellow fever to the community. How could anyone possibly blame me when neither incident had anything to do with the people from the train?" Lydia fumed as she nearly side-swiped a horse and buggy. To her dismay, the person she had almost run into was none other than the Mayor of Waycross, Mr. Blake Thornesby himself.

"Whoa," he called to his two silky black Standardbreds, his whip held high in the air. The two horses pranced to a stop with a loud snort and a shake of their manes that ended with a stomp of their hooves.

"What in Sam Hill?" The Mayor's mutton chops seemed to quake beneath his huge jowls. "Is that you, Miss Lydia?" he asked, squinting into the sunlight. "And are you driving... a motor car?"

"It is, and I sure am. Isn't it grand?" she added to which she merely received a puff of air from the jowly Mr. Thornesby that made his chin quiver like a bowl of mint aspic.

"Well, I believe you could use another lesson or two, am I right Mr. Henderson?"

Rex–the traitor–laughed uproariously, then put his hands up in apology. "You must admit, Miss Lydia, you're *not* the best driver on the block, but I'm certain, with time, you'll come to own the road."

"I may not be the *best* driver, Mr. Henderson, but right now I am the *only* driver," Lydia said to which they both laughed.

"Touché," Rex said.

The mayor, who was known to be dour at best, sullen at worst, had an amused glint in his eye. "Maybe it's the shoes that are giving you trouble," he suggested, pointing to the wedged heels she had found in the attic earlier that day, which brought on even more peals of laughter from the two men until finally, she sighed.

"Well, good day, sir." She was about to let the mayor pass when a thought came to her. "Wait, Mayor Thornesby."

The whip was held high in preparation for departure, but the mayor paused, as though a conductor preparing for the orchestra to play but awaiting an errant flutist or oboist who had yet to turn to a new score.

"Did you happen to see today's headlines?" Lydia said, unable to hide the anger in her voice.

His dark bushy brows hovered like a storm cloud above his eyes. "That I did."

"How can anyone possibly believe this drivel? And what can I do about it?"

"One thing you must understand, Miss Lydia, a town needs a scapegoat when crises occur. Fear drives people to unimaginable atrocities. We have only to look at the Civil War to see the truth in that."

Or to Banjo Peavy, Lydia thought, or to John Brown, who was lynched because he was said to have scared a white girl. Still, although the mayor was more tolerant than some, Lydia thought it wise to remain silent. She was already in enough hot water.

A surrey pulled up behind the mayor and the driver jingled a bell that hung from his callash to urge them on their way.

"I know I may have seemed harsh the other day on your lawn,

but I have to answer to constituents. Come to my office... no, better yet, stop by the house the day after tomorrow... after dark. Maybe we can find a way out of this... mess."

The bell that hung from the fringe-topped canopy of the surrey trailing the mayor once again jingled and the roan from the one-horse cart stamped its frustration.

"I'll be off then," the mayor said, donning his stovepipe hat.

"I'll be there... and thank you," Lydia said, then waited as the two carriages passed before proceeding.

By the time they arrived home, Lydia felt spent. Rex tipped his hat slightly, then made his way to the carriage house via the side yard. As she entered the house through the back door, Webster ran to greet her, whereupon she quickly fed him. Then she let him into the backyard to explore the recent gopher holes that had begun to spring up in her beautiful green lawn, much to her dismay. The holes were a hazard of living so close to an open field which ran the perimeter of an especially large lot that abutted the backyard.

All manner of fruit trees dotted the adjacent lot, along with a very substantial vegetable garden and a row of loganberries that had been strung along a wire fence. The property had at one time been owned by her father, but it had been sold off after The Civil War to stave off financial calamity and to prevent either a carpetbagger or a scalawag from getting their hands on the family land. Still, she had fond memories of playing among the peach trees and the cherries that her father had planted, lo those many years ago, before the Greenwalds had installed a fence to keep the neighborhood kids from playing there.

Tired, Lydia left Webster to his own devices as she went to her bedroom, took off her shoes and put on her slippers, feeling immeasurable relief to have the tight-fitting wedged heels off, her feet finally able to breathe. Just then, the telephone rang.

"Who could that be?" she murmured, then rose to retrace her steps through the bathroom that led to the powder room and the foyer closest to the backyard, where the telephone was located. On the third ring, Lydia answered the phone.

"Oh, there you are," said Gladys.

Lydia was about to ask how things were going on Gladys's end, then to give her the news of the day, when Gladys's voice came through the wire sounding too high and too giddy. Something was definitely amiss, but Lydia didn't have a clue as to what, precisely.

"Are you okay, Gladys?"

"I have someone on the line to speak with you." The words Gladys spoke were just a bit too precise for Gladys's ordinary chatter, causing Lydia's hackles to rise. "Yes, a Mr. Benson."

Benson, Benson... where had Lydia heard that name before? Then it came to her. The Bensons had holdings in Atlanta. Very wealthy. Owned half of Atlanta, it was rumored, though she felt sure that was a huge exaggeration. She wondered if this could be one and the same, *the* Mr. Robert Benson, of the Hurley Bensons, their family owning cotton plantations where they had traded not only in cotton but had expanded to shipping, where the real wealth was made.

As if reading her mind, Gladys said, "Mr. Benson is here on business, aren't you Mr. Benson?"

He hemmed and hawed but finally said, "Yes, I am, and that's why I would like to speak with you, Miss McAllister. I wonder if we could meet, say, in a half hour?"

Lydia's mind raced. What on earth could a man of his stature want with the likes of her? Although Lydia's family had been well off, by some standards, they were not even in the ballpark much less the playing field when it came to the Bensons. She wasn't sure she would even be welcome in the *parking lot* of the ballpark, come to think of it.

"Where?" she finally said.

"The Grand Central Hotel. I'll wait for you in the lobby."

Lydia knew the one–a three-story brick and stucco hotel on Pendleton Street. Most of the passengers riding the rails stopped there, only now the place must look like a ghost town with no travelers allowed in or out. She had managed to get enough of a look at the *Waycross Sentinel* to discover that the Georgia State Board of Health had instituted a travel ban in or out of the area that was effective starting today. This meant that it was no longer just the Vigilance Committee haphazardly controlling the borders.

"Oh, and if you have a medical bag, please bring it," Mr. Benson added. Then he said a hurried goodbye before she could ask why.

"Hmm." Lydia tapped her chin with her forefinger then set about readying herself for the trip over. That meant that Mr. Benson had somehow managed to come through prior to the ban.

She quickly told Rex about her curious conversation with Mr. Benson. And even though she felt nervous about driving alone, she encouraged Rex to rest after such a long eventful day.

"Miss Lydia," Rex said as delicately as possible, "right now, you're a danger to society in that automobile of yours. I'm coming with you."

He made it clear he would allow no opposition, and truth was, she was glad to have him as extra eyes and ears. It was hard enough learning the fundamentals of driving without having someone to warn her of a coming intersection or a horse-drawn carriage, or a simple pedestrian, for that matter. She quickly put on her boots, wishing suddenly that women's footwear was more practical, more comfortable. But she couldn't complain. In her mother's day, the left shoe and the right shoe had been identical in shape and must have been much more uncomfortable than they were now. She felt grateful for the new design that differentiated between the two. At least now, she didn't have two left feet!

Moments later, they were once again on the road, only this time heading into town instead of away from it.

"What do you suppose we'll find when we get there?" Rex asked, the gray stubble on his chin glistening in the waning light.

"Something that involves my medical bag," she said, giving him a long, meaningful look.

"Watch out, Miss Lydia!" Rex cried just in time for her to swerve to keep from hitting a hansom cab head-on. It was followed by much shouting.

Lydia pulled the car over and parked, her hands quaking on the steering wheel. Several minutes passed before she realized they had arrived at the Grand Central Hotel, and hence the cab. Rex exited the car then ran to her side of the vehicle to offer her his hand. Then together they walked toward the tall glass doors.

For one brief moment, Lydia was a child again, holding her mother's hand as they entered the hotel to collect Rose, who had just returned by train from a medical conference. Then as now, the inside of the lobby sported red Turkish carpets, which set off the rich mahogany of the main entry desk. Plush chairs sat among Sago palms with a vase-like spittoon in one corner and a bank of mirrors against the wall. But instead of Rose, a tall, thin man, who was both handsome and worldly in appearance, paced the carpet. His vest was of the finest grey silk, his smoke-colored jacket lying on a nearby chair, his dark hair gleaming with pomade and his mustachioed face tanned.

"There you are!" he cried, his eyes resting on her medical bag. He leaned close and spoke softly so that no one else would hear what he had to say. "I need your help. I'll explain as we take the elevator."

He led her to an ornate gated elevator with a wheat seed grill and a half-dome of etched brass that arched over it. He opened the elevator and ushered them both in, then closed it behind them and pushed the button, whereupon it rattled its way to the third floor as he explained the emergency.

"You see, my Diana is ill," Mr. Benson said, worry lines etching his forehead, sweat glistening his brow. "I believe she has yellow fever. I knew if anyone could help, it would be you."

And so, there it was, the crux of the matter. The man's wife was sick, possibly dying, and he hadn't known where to turn. No doubt he had read the article in the *Waycross Sentinel* and thought Lydia might be a potential ally. But the truth is, she was a poor substitute for a doctor.

"You must understand," she said, "I'm not a trained medical professional, but I'll do my best."

"Fair enough," he replied.

Yet he'd spoken in such an enigmatic way that Lydia couldn't help but think he was hiding something. After all, why Lydia? Why not a real doctor for someone of his stature and wealth? She had a feeling she would soon learn the reason.

The elevator jostled them as it screeched to a halt on the top floor. They emerged into a long hallway and hurried north along the corridor until they reached a room with a brass nameplate that read Room 301.

"Before you go in," Mr. Benson said, "there's something I should tell you. Something you need to know." He glanced nervously between the two of them, his dark eyes pleading for understanding.

"Go on, Mr. Benson," Lydia said. "I'm listening."

"Diana, you see–"

"Yes?"

He fidgeted with his hands, looking right and left, anywhere except in Lydia or Rex's eyes. "You see, Diana is my mistress. She's not my wife."

20

From the Archives of Joan Elaine Fields, M.D.:

"Sleepwear in the late 1800s for women has changed little since the early 1800s. For women in upper-class circles, this means full-length gowns usually made of cotton and sometimes silk and lace. Whereas for men, a new sleepwear called pajamas has been introduced in hopes of replacing the typical nightshirt and nightcap that are still the predominant clothing for nighttime. In 1880, pajamas were introduced from India and derived from the Hindi word. It consists of a short shirt and pants, usually cotton but sometimes silk. Can you imagine a woman ever wearing pajamas? What will they think of next?"

AUNT ROSE'S FASHION FAUX PAS

When Mr. Benson opened the door to the hotel room, Lydia walked into what could only be described as a luxurious room with rich red brocade drapes and posh Turkish rugs. What struck her most, however, was the honey-blonde woman in the silk lace peignoir who seemed dwarfed by the huge four-poster bed that stood in the middle of the room. Despite the sweat on her brow and the jaundiced appearance of both her face and eyes, it was clear to see that Diana was both cultured and beautiful, reminding Lydia of Lillian Russell whose name was synonymous with American operettas. Like Miss Russell, Diana had porcelain features and soulful eyes. It was also clear to see by the worry lines on Mr. Benson's face that he was smitten with the young ingenue.

"How long has she been like this?" Lydia asked, already opening her bag and pulling out a thermometer, which she quickly inserted into the woman's small mouth.

"Two days."

Dwarfed as she was in the king-sized bed, Diana looked like a small, sick child who had stayed home from school.

"Why didn't you call someone before now?" Lydia demanded, her temper flaring.

Rex steadied her with a hand on the shoulder.

"I was afraid." He latched onto Diana's hand and gave it a desperate squeeze, as though by the mere act of holding it he could bring her back to health.

"It has clearly gone to her liver. She's going to need a doctor. A *real* doctor," Lydia said, hoping he understood the severity of the situation.

At that, Mr. Benson crumpled into the chair that stood next to the bed, his hand still in Diana's. He lay his forehead against her pale fingers as though pleading forgiveness, a man of high stature brought low by a competitor he could not fight. Yellow fever. As she knew only too well, it ravaged not only the poor and uneducated, it brought the mighty low, as well. It held no bias in its ruthlessness. It was, in a word, the great equalizer.

Lydia removed the thermometer from the woman's mouth and read it. One-hundred four degrees. Rex passed her a guarded look that reflected hers.

"Mr. Benson, we *must* call a doctor."

"You don't understand," he said with an anguished expression that revealed the fears warring inside him, "it would ruin me if word got out."

Lydia walked over and bent down so that she stood eye to eye with Mr. Benson who smelled of cologne and cigars. She lay a hand on his arm in hopes of allaying his fears.

"I understand your concern, Mr. Benson, and I think I know a way that we can keep this just between us, but you're going to need to trust us."

For all his strength and renown, Robert Benson suddenly appeared humbled, almost boyish in his mannerisms. A shank of dark hair fell across his face so that he peered up at her with one eye.

"What can I do?"

Lydia glanced up at Rex who nodded his head, apparently having decided already that whatever she had planned he was on board.

"I need you to leave Diana with us for now, until we get her through this crisis."

"W-what?" he blustered, panic making his eyes turn a glassy brown. "I can't leave her."

"No!" Diana cried, her voice weak. Then she sank back onto the pillow and closed her eyes.

Taking his free hand and giving it a gentle squeeze of encouragement, Lydia said, "If not, you will put both her and yourself in jeopardy. Don't you see? Something like this can't be kept quiet for long. If the papers get hold of this—and sooner or later they will—you'll have no choice but to go public. Either that or you leave now and we will see that she's given the best chance possible to get well and to make a life for herself. It's up to you, but you must decide."

He jumped to his feet and began striding back and forth across the great expanse of room, stopping only to run a beleaguered hand through his hair and to curse at the fates that had led him here, to this room, to this position in his life.

"But I love her," he said, his voice that of a petulant child.

Lydia thought back to what she had read in the daily tabloids about Mr. Benson and his numerous dalliances. Diana had not been the first, and no doubt she would not be the last. But Lydia had also read that this man had been through much over the past several years, both in business and in his personal life–a child who had died in childbirth and an embezzling partner who had fled the country with Robert Benson's money lining his suitcases. It had been a decidedly bad few years for the man and she knew he was hurting.

"I promise you we'll take good care of Diana. We'll see that she gets the best treatment possible."

He stopped his pacing and once again sank into the chair, this time in defeat. For several minutes, he sat with pursed lips, staring at Diana. Finally, he nodded.

"What do you have planned?"

Lydia breathed out the air she hadn't realized she'd been holding and saw that Rex did the same.

"Take off your vest and bring me your jacket."

"Why?"

She ignored him. "Do you have any other clothing besides this that you could wear? I would like your pants and shoes, as well." Before Mr. Benson could register his surprise, Lydia turned to Rex. "You're about the same size as Mr. Benson, are you not?"

A slow smile formed on Rex's face. "I believe I *could* fill his clothing out rather well if I do say so myself," he agreed.

"Right, then. I would like both of you to change. Is there a back door to the hotel, Mr. Benson?" Lydia felt sure that he already knew the most discreet entrances and exits.

"Yes. The alleyway... where carriages enter."

"I suggest you change quickly and leave. Then Rex and I will call the doctor." Lydia was about to go in search of ice for the young woman's fever and to give the men time to switch clothing when she turned back to Mr. Benson. "I know this is none of my business–"

"You're right, this *is* none of your business." He rubbed his face and sighed. "I'm sorry. I didn't mean to snap at you. This has just been very difficult. Tell me. What is it you were going to say?"

It was Lydia's turn to feel abashed, but she pressed forward nonetheless. She knew that men with his status were often forced into arranged marriages to unite well-bred families and families with money.

"Marriages aren't always perfect."

"But?"

She shook her head. "Never mind. I'm out of line. It *is* your business."

This stopped him, and for one brief moment Lydia saw a flicker (of what?) cross his face. Understanding? Sadness? Loss?

Embarrassed, she quickly busied herself. "I need to get something to cool Diana's fever," she said. Then she left them to do as they would, while she worked diligently to save the young woman's life.

21

From the Archives of Joan Elaine Fields, M.D.:

"Uniforms define us whether they be that of an aproned nurse, the jodhpurs used in riding, khakis or Naval whites worn for military purposes, or simply attire worn by a ballplayer. Whether we wear rags or the finest silk, our clothing reveals something about us. But it cannot reveal everything, for each of us is unique. Good people come in all shapes and sizes, in all colors of the rainbow, and wear all kinds of clothing. The same is true for people with more nefarious intentions. Therefore, it is important to look at each person as an individual. To hold those we love dear, and to hold at bay those who do not have our best intentions at heart. If we do this, our lives will be much happier."

AUNT ROSE'S FASHION FAUX PAS

Lydia walked down to the lobby and asked that a messenger be sent to Doc Henry to let him know that it was urgent that he come soon. For the next half hour, she waited in the lobby. Finally, she gave up the vigil and returned to the hotel suite.

When she entered, Mr. Benson was just finishing up his tearful goodbyes to the pale woman in the canopied bed.

"You'll want to be sure to quarantine yourself for the next two weeks so you don't risk spreading the disease to others," Lydia said, placing a hand on his arm.

Mr. Benson appeared stricken but then nodded. "I have a home in the Hampshires that I can use. I can release a statement to the press saying that I'm in need of a rest after a very difficult year. It's the truth, at any rate."

"How will you get through the blockade?"

At that, he simply laughed. "That's *my* secret."

Either money or reputation would no doubt grease the wheels, of that she felt certain. With one final farewell to both her and Diana, who lay quietly sobbing, he dipped his hat to Lydia and left. Just in time, because no sooner had she stepped to the window to watch him exit the building and leave in a waiting coach, than she saw another carriage arriving from behind, carrying Doc Henry. He would know what to do.

Several minutes later, Lydia heard a knock at the door and walked over to answer it. There stood the thin wiry man with an aquiline nose and graying hair that everyone called Doc Henry. He had been called that for so many years that Lydia had forgotten his last name.

For some odd reason, he paused to take stock of her and she squirmed under his gaze. Then, wasting no further time, the doctor said, "Yellow fever?"

Lydia nodded as the man swallowed a short intake of air, blinked twice, then entered. He immediately commandeered the tabletop closest to her bed, turning it into a quasi-medical station. He sat his black bag on it, produced a tightly tatted cloth that he stretched out over the tabletop, then placed each of his pieces of equipment onto the clean cloth.

First, he wiped the end of his stethoscope with a tissue doused with alcohol, which he placed around his neck. Then he reached for a thermometer and shook it. With that done, he walked over and placed it in the young woman's still trembling mouth. As he warmed the metal end of the stethoscope on his hand, then placed it on the woman's chest, Lydia heard a knock on the door followed by the words "room service."

"That must be the ice," she said, absentmindedly.

"I'll get a towel to wrap it in," Rex offered.

"Thanks."

Lydia opened the door just enough to reach for the ice and to hand the man a small tip. She thanked him and was about to close the door when the bellhop said, "The manager thought he saw the doctor enter through the alleyway. Is there a problem that we should be aware of?"

Lydia froze. She hadn't counted on having to answer questions so soon. "Nothing to worry about. Our friend was just feeling a bit faint is all. I am sure she will be fine."

She knew that would keep the manager at bay just long enough for the doctor to make a thorough evaluation of the situation, which seemed fairly straightforward at this point.

Sure enough, no sooner had the doctor concurred that indeed the woman was suffering from yellow fever and began working to cool her fever when Lydia heard another knock at the door. All three–the doctor, Rex, and Lydia–stood staring at it. The pounding became more pronounced until the door virtually shook. Finally, they all sprang into action. Rex raced to the door and opened it, Lydia following close behind, while the doctor continued his ministrations.

The man who stood before them was dressed in a dark gray suit with a maroon vest and a watch fob. "I was told you have a woman in here who is ill, am I correct?"

Rex and Lydia exchanged glances. At that moment, Lydia decided not to mince words.

"She has yellow fever and the room–the entire wing–will have to be closed to visitors. Do you have a service elevator that we can disinfect when we are done using it?"

The concierge paled, the pencil mustache quivering ever so slightly. He parted his hair in the middle as was common in Paris, not Waycross, Georgia. The whites of his eyes circled his irises as if giving life to his fears.

The doctor, who had been silent up until now, said, "By law, we have the right... no, the *obligation* to keep the community safe. Therefore, if I must, I will call the sheriff to guarantee my rights as a doctor to safeguard the citizens of Waycross, Georgia."

If possible, the concierge paled further. At last, he clicked his heels together as if in acknowledgment of the truth.

"I'll see that the entire top floor is cordoned off. You may use the service elevator. It is on your right as you leave the hallway. It's locked, but I'll see that it is unlocked for the duration of your stay so that only you can use it. I ask only one thing."

"And that is?" Doc Henry said.

"That you tell no one of the woman's illness. It would ruin my business."

The doctor exchanged looks with both Lydia and Rex. When Lydia nodded her agreement, as did Rex, the doctor said, "You have my word. It will be between us."

The concierge seemed to swoon, but quickly regained his footing and thanked them profusely.

"One last thing..."

"Oh?" the doctor asked.

"Promise me there will be no death cart. Mort Shipke was taken away today and his wife Claudia may not be far behind. Please, promise me."

Lydia gasped, her eyes welling with the news. The poor Shipkes. They were such good people.

"I promise," the doctor said, offering his sympathy to Lydia with a brief nod.

What a horrible position for the doctor–for all of them for that matter–to have to bargain with death. To have to pray that they would remain healthy amidst all the fear and disease that seemed to go hand in hand whenever an unexplained illness arose. It was as if the primitive sides of people that lay lurking in the shadows suddenly came to the forefront–a need to protect one's own at the cost of all others outside the circle.

The concierge nearly collapsed with relief, bowed once, and then left in a scurry of movement. Rex closed the door behind him. In that simple act, it was as if the foursome left in this room were all on a lifeboat together with no timeline for rescue, no certainty that they would find shore. They had to rely on skill, faith, and simple luck. From now on, everything was out of their hands, except for that small bit of skill, however much that might, or might not, help.

Once they were all alone and had done everything they could for Diana, the doctor gathered up the items he had laid on the tabletop and placed them almost lovingly into his bag.

"Before I go," he said, lifting his bag off the counter. "I would like to talk to you two."

Lydia glanced at Rex, wondering if he knew what this was about, but he seemed just as confused as she.

"Please, take a seat," he said, and then sat on a silky green ottoman facing them. When they were all situated, he continued. "It's in my power to make both of you Health and Safety Auxiliary Members."

Lydia looked over at Rex, who appeared drained of color.

"This could get worse," the doctor proceeded. "Much worse."

"You know I have no formal training," Lydia said, determined to be upfront.

"Yes, I know. But I also know that your aunt Rose *was* a doctor. And a good doctor at that. She treated parts of the community that no one else would. In the world of medicine, she was quite unique–a woman in a man's world. In some circles, she is still considered heroic, in others, well... you know..." He looked down at his feet, unable to face Lydia.

Lydia's memory of Rose was somewhat jaded. She had been nineteen when Rose died of rheumatic fever after a bout of strep throat that she had failed to treat adequately, but she had been ill long before that.

To Lydia, Rose had been larger than life. As a child, Lydia had followed her around like a puppy dog. A smile came to her mouth unbidden at the nickname she'd garnered from some of the townsfolk: "Shadow." That was before Rose had lost her luster and, like the falling petals of a rose, had been ground into the dust of Waycross, Georgia's wiregrass country. Fortunately, Rose had benefactors who had helped her along the way, even during those difficult days when her aunt had been approached by the All White Council and "asked"–if there was such a thing–that she stop going across the tracks to help those of color. She hadn't. That, Lydia supposed, thinking back on it now, was when *Rose* became invisible, and Lydia soon afterward. No one would speak to the teenager. They would turn the other way when she or Rose went to town. An entire room would fall silent when they entered.

Still, it hadn't been all bad. Although Lydia had never received formal training, she had learned a lot at her aunt's side and had assisted her wherever she went.

"There's one thing you should know about me."

"Oh?"

"I'll help whenever I can," she said, "but I'm very independent. I'm afraid I'm not very good at taking orders. I suppose that comes from being raised mostly by Rose."

"Yes, I've been well aware of that since I learned of your recent... *exploits*." He raised a brow, and yet his eyes held a twinkle with just a bit of mirth dancing around his mouth.

Lydia turned to the very ill young woman in the bed. "What shall I do about Diana?" she asked with a sigh.

"Leave that to me. I've sent for a nurse to keep watch over her. She should be here any minute," he said, reaching down and checking a pocket watch he had attached to his belt loop by a gold chain.

Lydia started in surprise to see the locomotive on the front, an exact copy of Rose's watch. More than once, Lydia had wondered what happened to it. Rightly or wrongly, she had assumed that it had been buried with her.

"As for Miss Diana here," Doc Henry continued, "she's young and in prior good health. Her chance for recovery is good and she should go on to live a full productive life, no doubt, so not to worry." He gave her shoulder a squeeze as he stood, then shook Rex's hand.

No sooner had Doc Henry opened the door to take his leave, than the nurse arrived dressed in a simple white cotton shift with puffs on the shoulders and a wide vee-neck collar sewn onto the bodice. She had forgone the cap that nurses normally donned in favor of a slicked-back hairstyle with a spit curl at her forehead.

"Thank you for coming, Gretchen," Doc Henry said, ushering her in and reading Diana's vital signs before taking his leave.

Although Gretchen appeared not much older than Lydia herself, she had the confidence of a much older woman.

"Shoo now," she said, urging them all along. "I can handle things from here. And Cookie will be here to cover the night shift."

"Cookie?"

"The other nurse." As if to remind them once again that she could handle things and they were to be on their way, Gretchen waved a hand, shooing them like chickens toward the door.

Before either of the pair could offer a protest, Lydia found herself outside the door with Rex, headed down the back hallway toward the doctor, who was waiting for the elevator to arrive.

"Can I give you a ride into town?" Doc Henry asked.

"We have a motor car."

"A car?" The doctor shook his head. "Will wonders never cease."

* * *

The next day, when Lydia arose, still tired after the last few days' ordeals, she walked out onto the front porch to collect her daily newspaper. Her eyes caught on the headlines. "Robert Benson In Seclusion."

She read on: "After a difficult year of losses, Robert Benson will be going into seclusion. In the coming days, he will be taking up residence in his summer estate in the Hamptons, where he plans to regroup after a difficult year. He says he hopes to spend more time with his family in the new year. His wife of 18 years and his daughter will meet him at their vacation home in two weeks' time. In the meantime, he asks that the media respect his privacy."

Tears welled in Lydia's eyes. Maybe miracles could still happen after all.

22

From the Archives of Joan Elaine Fields, M.D.:

"The Edwardian Age has brought with it new and varied changes. Heavy petticoats and bustles have replaced crinoline and cage hoops, skirts now a trumpet bell shape. For men, little has changed between the two eras. Calf-length coats or single-breasted tweed jackets are common, as are the three-piece suits that are apt to reveal a waistcoat. Add to that a top hat and ascot, and any man seen in Waycross would be thought dapper indeed."

AUNT ROSE'S FASHION FAUX PAS

Lester Pester two by four, can't get through the kitchen door, be he rich or be he poor, Lester Pester two by four.

Lydia hadn't even realized that she'd been rolling the ditty around in her head as she laid out the material on the wide oak table in the sewing room until she stopped to take a look at her handiwork. She didn't know what had possessed her to want to try her hand at design. Maybe she just needed a diversion from the unsettling events of the past few days. Yet, as if to remind her of her worries, she pricked her finger, a tiny droplet of blood dotting her fingertip, then covered it with a tissue to avoid getting it on her dress.

"For heaven's sake!"

She opened her sewing drawer where she kept band-aids for just such an occasion. Removing the tissue, she quickly taped the band-aid over it, then wrapped another one around it to hold the first one in place. That done, she turned back to her work.

Fortunately, Gladys had called Lydia to let her know that Diana would be moved within the week and that Doc Henry believed she would live. That was good news.

Now, as Lydia finished up the first half of her newest design, she had to admit the effect was stunning. The gown was to be of the palest gray satin with a lace overlay, flowers weaved into the lace so that it crossed the top right bodice of the dress, only to meet up with the hem of the skirt on the left, a gap of tight-knit lace in between. She'd ordered the material from a house that purchased materials from all over the world, the lace from France.

The sleeves were capped, unseemly for the end of the Victorian Age to be sure, but if they were no longer in the Victorian Age, where were they precisely? The Edwardian Age, she supposed, with its blouses, skirts and crocheted bags, chandelier necklaces and platinum filigree as accents to an otherwise bland style, in her opinion.

She shook her head to clear the cobwebs, her thoughts drifting to Rex. He had proved to be a stalwart companion over the past week. With good food and regular baths, his gaunt, craggy features were filling in and he was becoming quite handsome. Truth was, he seemed like a new man. He no longer peered down at his feet when talking to her, rather he looked her square in the eye. They had developed a mutual respect, and for that, she felt grateful.

She pulled out pins from her red velvet pincushion, its filigreed stand made of a sardine tin that Rex had found and made into what looked like a rocking chair fit for a palace, replete with two hearts entwined to form the back of the chair. Tramp art, they called it. She didn't know why, but she thought it the loveliest gift she had ever received. It was as if he, of all people, had seen inside her, knew who she really was and had not found her lacking in some way.

How many times throughout her life had she heard, "Oh Lydia, you would be so pretty if you just did your hair another way." Or "Oh Lydia, you really should wear something more flattering to your figure." Or better still, "Lydia, have you ever considered a corset? It would hide your excess middle." No one had ever said that she was smart, funny, kind. No one had ever seen that beauty wasn't just layered onto the surface like a fine veneer. If a woman weren't flawless, they were cast aside. She had seen it time and time again. It was part of the reason she had shied away from men.

No, she had heard too many rumors about the various husbands around town and the idea of ending up with a lothario and becoming the talk of the town socials had scared her. On the flip side of the coin, she'd seen beautiful women do and say things that would have buried someone of lesser qualities.

On a sigh, she stood and glanced out the upstairs window, stretching her back to work out the kinks. She was just about to return to work when she heard the rattle and clack of one of the death carts. She screeched, then ran down the stairs, running straight into Rex's arms.

"Whoa there, Missy."

"You heard it?"

"I did," he said in that low baritone of his. "Who do you suppose it is? I only knew of Mort and Claudia."

She shook her head. "I don't know. But I aim to find out."

Rex put a steadying hand on her shoulder. "Let's find out together," he advised, to which she nodded. It would help to stay calm.

Already, people were flocking to their doors, watching the slow procession in something that could only be described as horror. Besides Lydia and Rex, the judge, who normally worked during the week, was one of the few to venture out on the street.

"Who has died?" Lydia asked the judge as the death cart rattled past.

The judge pursed his lips, his caterpillar brows furrowed in consternation. He was nearing sixty and was just beginning to gray at the temples of his nearly jet black hair.

"Apparently, the Peabody's aunt and uncle got through the cordon. They were on the train. No one knows exactly how the Peabodys snuck them off the train under darkness. Rumor has it they had help from someone in this area."

"Which of the Peabodys is on the cart?" Lydia's heart was racing, so much so that she prayed he wouldn't see it beating through her blue crinoline dress.

"Peabody's aunt, I've heard. The uncle seems healthy enough, but they're taking no precautions. Mr. Peabody's family will be quarantined from this point on." The judge tugged at his chin, his dark eyes alight with curiosity. Dubbed "the pit bull," he was known to pursue a case until every last shred of evidence was found, as long as that evidence favored the white community.

"What will happen to the Peabodys?" Rex asked.

"Charges may be drawn up," the judge said absentmindedly, his thoughts clearly on the cart rattling by and the potential ramifications.

"You can't do that!" Lydia blurted before thinking through what she had said.

The judge turned to her, his focus no longer on the death cart. One eyebrow shot up and he pinned her with a look that was both suspicious and curious at the same time.

"And why *can't* I do that?" he asked, folding his arms across his chest and leaning toward her, making her feel instantly intimidated.

"Well, it's just that they're such a nice family. They work hard. People do make mistakes you know."

"Do they?" Again, he affixed her with a stare that made her want to wither in the noonday heat.

Rex reached out and grabbed Lydia's elbow. "The show is over," he said, nodding to the judge who dipped his head and walked across the street to his large craftsman-style home with the wide porch and rock stanchions.

They turned to go when, suddenly, they saw Millie Harper running toward them, her face blotchy and red.

"This is your fault, Lydia McAllister! You helped those people. I know it. We all know it." With that, she turned on her heel and left.

Despite the heat, Lydia felt a shiver run up her arms. Rex put his hand on the small of her back and urged her toward the house. The driveway had never felt so long. Once inside, she began trembling, her knees feeling as though they might buckle.

"Come, sit," Rex said. "I'll fix you a sarsaparilla, or would you rather have lemonade?"

"I have some lemonade already made up," she said, still reeling from her conversation with both the judge and Millie.

Moments later, he returned carrying two hand-painted pink tumblers with miniature roses painted on the glass. He plunked one down in front of her, then took a seat beside her.

"Quick, take a sip. It'll cool you off."

She felt like a child, and yet it was comforting to have someone else take charge for once. It had been so long since she'd had any companionship. She took a long swig of the tart juice, then set the glass on the table covered in white lace.

"What do you think will happen... with the judge, I mean?" Lydia asked, still reeling from her conversation with the elderly man.

"Let's just hope he's busy elsewhere," he said, mysteriously, then took a sip of his lemonade.

She paused before his meaning became clear. "You mean with the Vigilance Committee?"

"Precisely," he said, placing a paper napkin beneath both tumblers.

"What makes you think he'll do anything about them? After all, they've bullied the townsfolk for years."

He ran a finger across the rim of his glass. "Let's just say I hear a lot on the streets."

Lydia frowned at the mention of him living on the streets. "I hope you won't think me nosy, Mr. Henderson–"

"It's time you called me Rex, ma'am," he said, drumming his fingers on the table.

"Rex. And please, call me Lydia."

He shrugged his shoulders and grimaced. "How about we make a deal. I'll call you Lydia in private and you can call me Rex, but in public, you will be Miss Lydia and I will be Mr. Henderson."

"Deal." They shook hands on it, then Lydia laughed. It felt good to laugh. Lately, there had been so little reason for laughter.

"So, Rex," she said, tentatively, "if you don't mind my asking, how did you end up on the...?"

"Streets?" he offered.

"Yes," she said on an exhale.

"You'll laugh at this, but as I'm sure you know, I'm from the other side of the county. Back in '96, I went to Harvard. I was in law school, believe it or not. Graduated top of my class."

The fan hummed in the silence that followed, the large teal wall clock ticking in accompaniment to her thoughts.

"Then how did you end up..." she held her hands out, her eyes darting around as if to say "here."

"It's a long story."

"I have time."

He dipped his head in frustration, but seeing that she had no intention of terminating this line of questioning, he said, "I studied International Humanitarian Law. Before I could go into practice, I was drafted into service for the Spanish-American War under McKinley. I was commissioned into the U.S. Navy and was sent to Cuba under Dewy. I fought in the battle of Manila Bay."

Although Lydia had heard of the war, it seemed a distant beast, something that until now had no connection to her whatsoever. And she supposed that was the way of things–until a war affected one personally, it was difficult to understand, to relate.

"Your family's rich," she said, stating the obvious.

"So why was I drafted?" he asked with a wry chuckle.

She nodded.

"Oh, my parents would have done anything to keep me out of the war, or at the very least to be assigned to a prime post, but I couldn't do it." He wiped the wet ring that his glass had left on the cream-colored lace. "How could I practice Humanitarian Law if it didn't apply to me?"

"Mmm," she said, fingering the moisture beaded on the side of her glass. "What happened then?"

He tapped his drink on the tabletop, his eyes distant, as though recalling an earlier time. "We came home with a high number of what they termed 'mentally ill' veterans of the war. People thought it was a result of being exposed to cannon fire. One of the officers, John Pershing, thought it was due to concussive injuries to the brain as a result of being exposed to such loud explosions. He called it 'shell-shock'." He shrugged his shoulders again. "I guess the name stuck."

Lydia snorted. "Mentally ill. So suffering emotional trauma is a mental illness now? If that were the case, then most of us would be mentally ill at some point or another in our lives," she said, recalling those long days after Rose died, then her parents. She had wanted to curl up in a ball in her room and never come out again. If it hadn't been for the family lawyer urging her to deal with financial matters, she might have never left her room. But she had to eat, and she had to secure the estate by filling out miles of paperwork, much of it redundant. Over time, she had realized that the house and the yard needed tending. Slowly but surely, she had returned to the world of the living, but that first year had been a muddle of tears and frustration. But most of all, loneliness.

Rex chewed his lower lip.

"Do you believe *you* are mentally ill?" Lydia took his hand and forced him to look her in the eye. "Do you?"

"I'm wounded, I'll grant you that, but mentally ill?" He shook his head.

Lydia felt a simmering anger in the pit of her stomach. As a child, working with Rose, she'd gone to places and had seen things that no person should have to see. She supposed it was what gave her such empathy for the underdog. She had seen children starved, caged like animals, no more mentally ill than anyone else, but they responded to abuse in the only way they knew how by lashing out or melting down into a puddle of tears. It was normal. It was *human*.

"For who among us has not suffered?" Lydia said, quoting her aunt Rose. "But that's the thing–some suffer more than others. Suffer so that the rest of us don't have to. And then they–"

"Throw us out on the street?"

"Exactly."

"You have to understand," he said, pulling his hand away from hers and appearing timid suddenly. "They didn't throw me out on the street. I went willingly."

Lydia drew her hand back. "But why?"

"Because I no longer had faith in mankind. I saw things–*did* things–that no human being should ever see or do. Can you understand? I trusted people to be decent, to be caring. But maybe, in the end, we're just savage animals, no better or worse than any other animal."

"You can't mean that," she said, pushing the rose-colored glass aside.

"Oh, but I do. You see, when people are afraid, or are allowed power without restraint, all pretense of civilization is gone."

They sat in silence for several moments until Lydia had a thought, a question. "But you trusted me enough to stay. Why?"

He tapped the table with his fingers as though the answer lay somewhere beneath them. "When I heard what you were doing, I knew if I could ever trust anyone, it would be you."

"You heard what I was doing? Before I found you in the alley? By whom?"

Rex lifted his head with a sly smile that overshadowed his earlier sadness. "From Gladys."

Lydia sat straighter in her seat. "Gladys? How on earth?"

"Well, things may not have gone as smoothly as she let on at the train station. See, some very angry men were set to go after her when they saw her try to drive away. I had heard about what they were planning and had already prepared a diversionary tactic of my own. I gathered a bunch of tree limbs and stacked them high. I set a bonfire." He laughed, his eyes appearing far away, as if to another night, another time.

"You saved her?"

He chuckled. "Let's just say I gave her a head start out of that place... put a fiery branch between them and her."

"Why Mr. Henderson–"

"Rex," he said, offering her a sly look.

"Rex. You, my sir, are a scoundrel." She looked at him with new respect.

"It appears that we both have a bit of that in us, does it not?"

"Indeed." She smiled. "Maybe I'll have that sarsaparilla after all." When he had refilled their glasses, they clinked them together. "Cheers!"

Yet minutes later, even as she sipped on the cool sarsaparilla, she couldn't help feeling uneasy as though a shadow had just crossed over her, as though the spirit of some ancestor had run through her on its way toward disaster. It was the feeling she'd had when her mother had died, that ebullient woman who had seemed too full of life for anything to ever befall her. Lydia had felt it again when her aunt Rose had died, the feeling was so unlike any other. Most times, when she thought of her aunt, a warm glow filled her with a love so deep that she wished she could capture it and save it, like fireflies in a mason jar on a warm summer night. But this feeling was decidedly different.

"It'll be okay, Lydia," Rex said, as though reading her thoughts.

"How do you know?" she countered.

"I suppose I don't know for sure." He offered her a sheepish glance. "But I do know one thing–"

"Oh?"

"Life is easier when you're not alone."

For just a second, she thought she had seen a glint of moisture in his eyes, but then he tightened his jaw and sat taller.

"That it is," she agreed. "That it is."

23

From the Archives of Joan Elaine Fields, M.D.:

"During times of disaster, it's best to stay calm, not to worry about what one looks like to others because they don't know us. They only see the exterior, assign us with intentions that mirror their own rather than see us for who we really are."

AUNT ROSE'S FASHION FAUX PAS

Lydia, Lydia, Lydia. Clang, clang, clang. In her dream, the telephone was ringing and Rose had been trying to shake Lydia awake. She blinked and sat up in bed. It took a moment to get her bearings, and a moment further to realize the telephone was indeed ringing. She stood up too quickly, her head reeling. To steady herself, she held onto the pineapple finial of the four-poster bed until her blurred vision cleared.

She donned her robe and slipped her feet into satin slippers, then she tore down the stairs and lifted the receiver of the telephone just in time to hear the words "Sorry I missed you."

"Gladys, is that you?" she said in a rush, hoping Gladys hadn't hung up.

"Oh, Lydia, thank goodness I caught you."

Lydia glanced over at the banjo clock on her kitchen wall. 5:30 A.M. What could Gladys possibly want at this hour? Whatever it was, it couldn't be good.

"What is it?

"Oh, Lydia. Some weisenheimer set the Peabodys' house on fire."

Lydia couldn't breathe. The clanging in her dream hadn't been the phone. It had been the horse-drawn fire engines racing to the fire. Rex must have heard it too because he hurried up the steps that led to the back porch from his room dressed in her father's robe and slippers, his hair askew.

He flung the door open. "What is it? What happened?"

She put her hand over the mouthpiece and whispered, "A fire, at the Peabodys' home."

"I'll get dressed," he said. "How soon can you be ready?"

"I'll hurry." Lydia thanked Gladys for calling her, then said a quick goodbye.

Normally, Lydia loved this time of the morning when the sun kissed the horizon and the smell of freshly mown lawns scented the air, setting her mind at ease. Today, however, her thoughts turned with sadness to Mr. Peabody. The Peabodys would be homeless if the volunteer fire department couldn't save their home. Well, she could do nothing about it standing around here, moping.

She gathered her belongings, then rushed to meet Rex, who had finished dressing and was waiting for her next to the garage. As she climbed into the motorcar, she thought of the fear that had become rooted in the hard clay soil of Waycross, sprouting in a violence that had begun to sweep through the town like kudzu, a vine that could grow a foot a day.

What's wrong with people?

The Peabodys had been beloved by all. Mr. Peabody was an elder at the church, and Mrs. Peabody was the first to bring trays of food for anyone in need. If the town could turn on the Peabodys, they could turn on anyone. Lydia pulled her lace scarf tighter around her chin as Rex cranked up the engine. The motor sputtered, then coughed, finally churning to life with one last puff of smoke. He jumped in, not even bothering to shut the garage door.

Ten minutes later, they turned left onto Gilmore Street, the sight of people stopping and staring at the motor car now familiar to Lydia. On Gilmore, they passed a beautiful Queen Anne with its wide front porch and neatly trimmed boxwoods, which acted as a border to another old Victorian that showcased two large palmettos and a wrought iron gate. The area had a bucolic feeling, as though it ran on a completely different timetable than that of Atlanta, the nearest large city, which ran at a frenetic pace even in the best of times.

But Lydia had no time to dwell on such thoughts, for dawn was quickly giving way to daylight and with it, the smell of burning embers. Lydia covered her mouth with the hem of her long overcoat as they neared. Smoke, which had begun as a gray haze, now roiled toward them, as people poured from their homes and lined the street to watch the firemen work desperately to save the large wood-framed home.

"Pull over," Lydia urged.

Rex tried but was forced to park the car in the street due to lack of space next to the sidewalk as nearly half the town, it would seem, had gathered to see the commotion.

In stunned silence, Lydia watched as gray smoke turned to black. Unlike the earlier Victorians they had passed on their way here, this home was done in the Georgian Colonial style of the early 1800s. It was no doubt one of the original homes in the area. Already, Lydia could see flames licking at the eight windows, four on the lower story, four on the top story, smoke billowing out the front door of the rectangular structure. The paired brick chimneys stood like twin gashes in the morning sky, arms reaching to the heavens in supplication. But the plea would go unheeded today, for it was easy to see that whatever hope of salvation might have been offered, provided sufficient time, had now lapsed. The best that could be hoped for at this moment was that the family had escaped and were now watching the conflagration at a safe distance.

"Have you seen the Peabodys?" Lydia asked Rex as she craned to see above the heads of the crowd.

With a beleaguered sigh, Rex said, "Not a one."

In grim fascination, they watched as flames licked at the blackened exterior of the home, crackling and popping as the structure turned in on itself. All the while Lydia prayed that the family was safe, that Mr. Peabody had started his rounds early and that Mrs. Peabody was elsewhere, visiting relatives perhaps, or fleeing to a safer spot.

"If we ask the firemen, do you think they'll tell us if the family made it out safely?" she asked, now that it had become clear that all hope was lost of saving even the smallest section of the home, its wood a tinderbox for the hungry flames.

"Only one way to find out," Rex said, opening the door to his side of the motor car.

Lydia scrambled to exit the vehicle, hoping against hope that the Peabodys were even now safely on the lawn, dirty from the soot but alive. Most of all, alive.

Rex grabbed her hand. No sooner had they pressed their way to the front of the crowd when a fireman shouted, "Stay back!

Everyone back!"

A loud crack was followed by a groan as the house seized in upon itself. Like one of the grand old Andalusian horses Lydia's forebears had owned, the Georgian home appeared to sit down on its haunches as first one side collapsed in slow motion, then the other, so that it seemed to have lain down completely, the blackened window on the left side of the building looking like a single closed eye.

The crowd, which at first had let out a collective gasp followed by a loud murmur that rose in waves, now fell silent. The only sound was the fire licking at the remains of the burned-out building. Even the firefighters seemed to have succumbed to the inevitable and stood back as God and nature took their course.

Rex squeezed Lydia's hand tightly even as tears brimmed his eyes. At that moment, Lydia wondered what fires Rex had seen in the Spanish-American War, what memories even now licked at the house of his mind, attempting to tear down the feeble structure that he had built since the war to keep him sane.

She squeezed his hand and held on tightly before letting go.

At that moment, one of the firemen tramped out onto the lawn and fell to his knees, smoke steaming off him in waves, his face covered in soot. He removed his helmet and wept. Lydia gave Rex's hand one final squeeze then rushed over to the fireman and knelt down beside him.

"I couldn't save them," he cried, head in hands. "I tried."

"I know you did," Lydia said, embracing him and resting his head on her shoulder. "You did everything you could. This isn't your fault."

He was so young... so young to carry such a huge burden on his slender shoulders.

Behind her, Lydia heard a commotion and turned in time to

time to process the words, much less their meaning, which were unfathomable at any rate.

Finally, silence prevailed, and addressing the entire room very formally, Lonnie said, "This is She Who Sees Beyond the Veil, my mother. She is a great medicine woman of my people. She asks that she may help the little one with our Creator's medicine."

"You ladies heard that?" Paw-paw nearly shouted from his place on the bed. "What do you have to say for yerselves? You want'n this here medicine woman to help the young'un?"

Lydia exchanged glances with Harmony, her wide eyes revealing her desperation to help her son. At last, she nodded. With that, the woman knelt and placed a piece of cloth that she had brought with her onto the floor. Next, she opened up her pouch and placed sage, willow bark, a reddish brown crystal with twin crosses, and what looked like black bear teeth onto the swatch of cloth.

Inside another smaller pouch lay a mixture of pungent herbs. These, she handed to Sage as she spoke urgently. To Lydia's surprise, he understood her and set to work preparing a tea for the boy. While it was brewing, the Chickasaw woman said a prayer to each of the earth's four directions.

"She's giving thanks to the Creator," Lonnie said in a tone of quiet reverence.

Next, she pulled out a piece of flint and a small pouch of leaves at her side, followed by a flat stone with a dark center. She lay the leaves in the middle of the stone and napped the flint until it sparked, setting the leaves aglow. Once she had accomplished that, she took a piece of sage and lit it. With that, she began to dance toward the boy. It was then that Lydia noticed the bells on the woman's moccasins, each bell made of a shell with a small stone inside.

An inner light lit the woman's face and gave it a golden halo that caused Lydia to blink to be sure she hadn't dreamt it. Harmony must have noticed it too, for she stared agog at the healer, too entranced to question the odd ritual. By this time, Chester had begun drooling, his forehead beaded with sweat and the tremors growing stronger until Harmony let out a gasp and covered her mouth with her arm to keep from screaming in frustration at her inability to help her son.

They had all been so caught up by the medicine woman's strange chanting and the boy's escalating tremors that no one noticed that the chanting had abruptly stopped until Sage handed She Who Sees Beyond the Veil an old cup made of engraved pewter containing a strange smelling brew.

She thanked him in her language and knelt next to Chester, whose mouth lay open, his eyes unseeing. For a fearful moment, Lydia thought that perhaps Chester was dead, but the woman lifted his head with such a gentle, loving gesture that it was all Lydia could do not to cry. In a voice both soft and earnest, the woman spoke, her words filled with clicks and clacks, like a train as it ground into motion.

Moments later, to Lydia's amazement, the boy's eyes fluttered open. A murmur arose throughout the room like the mumble of bees that had felt a breeze and had reacted to the disturbance from their morning of lazy feeding in the noonday sun.

With a great thirst, Chester gulped down the warm liquid despite both his mother and the medicine woman's protests. Then he was soon fast asleep, his breathing no longer labored and his tremors subsiding.

An uneasy relief seemed to fill the silence as they watched and waited to see which way the wheel would turn. Would Chester live? Or would he die? Lydia prayed that he would live.

Next, the medicine woman turned her attention to Harmony. She called to Sage, who promptly filled a small cup with a clear fluid–moonshine, Lydia suspected, by the smell of it. Harmony drank it down with a grimace. Afterward, the woman turned to Lonnie and said something indecipherable. He rushed outside while she cleaned Harmony's ankle then realigned it. Harmony let out a sharp cry, her body going rigid just as Lonnie returned with a flat piece of wood.

Sage, who had been watching the medicine woman work and listening intently to her instructions, brought a large strip of cotton followed by a long strip of rawhide to tie around the ankle. Once she had the leg set, she gave Harmony another sip of the moonshine and urged her to rest.

For nearly the entire day, Lydia and the others sat talking amongst themselves in hushed whispers, allaying the boredom and worry only to relieve themselves or to stretch stiffened legs. And still, Chester slept on.

Lydia was helping Sage prepare the evening meal when they heard a rustle of noise outside. Lydia peered out in time to see two men riding an ass. The pair pulled up next to the railing and climbed down. Just behind them were Rex and Styles, who had stayed behind to try to retrieve the motor car from the ravine. Lydia clapped her hands and immediately felt repentant when she saw Chester stir, because there, to her never-ending joy, she saw Rex, and he was driving her motor car.

31

From the Archives of Joan Elaine Fields, M.D.:

"Today, I learned about Chickasaw weddings when I was called to aid a young boy with rheumatic fever. It was here that a man came calling with a piece of calico as a gift for his future bride. If accepted, he would return in his finest clothing, his face painted in vermillion and other paints. He would then commune with the father alone, seated on a hide before taking supper and then entering the bridal chamber. Thus were they to be married."

AUNT ROSE'S FASHION FAUX PAS

Lydia gazed through the glazed front window of the cabin at the setting sun, the scent of pine and earth rich with the pungent odor of falling leaves from the open window in the back of the cabin. She tapped her toe impatiently as she waited for the doctor to dismount his horse, and for Rex and Sage's brother, Styles, to exit the Ford. Soon, the doctor's assistant climbed the steps onto the sagging porch.

Whenever Lydia had pictured the new doctor's assistant, who was rumored to have joined the Waycross Hospital for Negroes just last month, she'd envisioned a man in his fifties with graying hair and a big black bag. So, it came as a surprise to her that the man was young, in his twenties, perhaps, or early thirties. He had a wide round face and was nearly the same height as her, and she stood five-foot-seven at best. Furthermore, he was white and pudgy, pasty almost. Lydia felt certain that if she poked him he would spring back like her mother's famous coconut cake, which she brought to most gatherings.

Lydia ran to the door and flung it open, allowing the last of the sunshine in before it would eclipse the mountain, shuttering the backwoods into darkness.

"You found us!" Lydia cried in relief.

One by one, she ushered the newcomers in. It would be a cramped night for all of them in the small rectangular log cabin as it was too late for any of them to travel on these warren of roads.

Rex was the last of the new arrivals to enter. Once inside, he introduced the doctor as Professor J. D. Fowler, who'd come all the way from Minnesota before arriving at Waycross, Georgia. For several minutes, Dr. Fowler greeted everyone and introductions were made.

The doctor proved to be an intelligent man who was nothing if not thorough. When he was done poking and prodding Chester, he turned to She Who Sees Beyond the Veil and said, "I don't know what you've done, but this boy appears to be on the mend. His fever has broken and his skin is beginning to regain pallor, from what you've told me."

As if to prove his point, Chester said, "I'm starving! When can we eat?"

Everyone laughed. While Sage prepared the meal, Dr. Fowler

hand.

Soon, Rex had the motor car running and they set out on the road again. Lydia's ears popped as they descended quickly, the city below now obscured by a chorus of trees. A half-hour later, the trees opened up and Lydia recognized the train tracks that led into town, one of six sets of tracks going in all directions.

"See?" Rex said. "Everything's normal."

Lydia had to admit that as they entered the city limits, the town appeared quite sleepy. Bees hummed lazily over the snapdragons and nasturtium. Most everyone appeared to have taken either to their screened porches or had opted to stay indoors to stave off the heat and humidity.

"You're right. I'm worrying about nothing." Rex winked at her and then tapped the bill of his brown driver's cap.

Lydia's cheeks felt warm. Now that they were almost home, she wondered how Webster had fared. She hadn't expected to be gone so long. Fortunately, she had left him outside with a large bowl of water, enough food to keep him fed for a day, and plenty of shade to keep him cool should he need it. Still, she had never left him outdoors overnight and she was anxious to see how he was faring.

"Almost there," Rex said, leaning back and yawning.

They had just turned a corner that would lead toward her section of town when she saw it. Yellow flags flying a warning. The death cart loaded with not just one body, but with several. She grabbed Rex's hand and held it until she feared she had drained it of all blood.

"Oh, Rex!" she cried. "Who now?"

32

From the Archives of Joan Elaine Fields, M.D.:

"Shoes are a defining feature and finish off any wardrobe, whether it be brown leather-and-suede mid-calves, or English cloth and patent leather boots with pearl buttons. Or perhaps simple black or white high-tops. Shoes allow us to bear even the roughest of roads by protecting our feet. Too tight and they can blister, too loose and they can chafe. So choose your shoes wisely lest they cause you pain. Care for them. Make them last. For shoes can be your best friend in a pinch (sorry for the pun!)."

AUNT ROSE'S FASHION FAUX PAS

By the time the large white Victorian "lady" appeared before Lydia, her thoughts were racing, yet she didn't have time to process what she'd witnessed moments earlier because there, pacing back and forth on Lydia's porch, was Gladys. She was dressed in a brown pencil skirt with a white puff-sleeved blouse. In her hand, she carried a Victorian sunbonnet, the wide lace tie trailing behind her. She wore high-heeled white boots with dozens of black eyelets running up the center of each.

"Uh-oh," Lydia said.

Rex pulled up in front of the house and stopped. "You go in. I'll park ole' Lizzie here out back."

Lydia thanked him and jumped out, nearly spilling onto the ground in her haste.

"Steady there, girl," Rex said, then tipped his hat and departed, the motor car backfiring as if in farewell.

Gladys's eyes caught Lydia's. She rushed down off the porch just as Lydia hurried to find out what had happened while she was gone.

"Oh, you're back. Thank God!" Gladys cried, taking Lydia's arm and steering her toward the house.

Disconcerted, Lydia fumbled her skeleton key into the lock. Finally, the heavy door creaked open and she rushed inside, Gladys hot on her heels.

Once inside and with the door shut, Lydia turned to her friend. "What happened? Is anything wrong?" But she knew the instant she saw the worry lines on Gladys's face that something was indeed wrong. *Very* wrong.

"You've got to leave. Gather up your things and go. Now!"

"Why? What has happened?"

Gladys covered her face with her hands and moaned. Lydia pulled her friend's hands away so she could speak to the distraught woman.

"Let me get you something to drink," she told Gladys, taking her arm and rushing her toward the kitchen where she had some cider for just such occasions.

Gladys stopped her in the dining room. "There's no time. The postal service has shut down and the town has been cordoned off. No one is allowed in or out, not even for work."

"What does that have to do with me?" Lydia asked, not understanding.

"The Vigilance Committee..." Gladys started, clearly out of breath.

Seeing an opening, Lydia once again took her friend by the arm and led her through the swinging saloon door to the kitchen, where she sat her down on one of the high-backed oak kitchen chairs before the poor girl fell down. Lydia reached inside the icebox for a pitcher of cider. Then she chose sweet tea for Rex and herself.

Once she had the glasses filled, she set them on the kitchen table. Then she brought over a plate of leftover lemon pound cake with a powdered sugar glaze and dished them onto three china plates before taking a seat. "Now take a sip of your drink, then tell me what's wrong."

"They *know*, Lydia," Gladys said, her voice choking with frustration.

"Know what, Gladys?" she said, taking the girl's hand and patting it.

"Know about you, about us, about the food and drink on the train."

"Yes, I know. Half the town came to my house the other day."

"You don't understand. They know about *everything*! Including the fact that you were with the bootleggers." Gladys put a fist to her mouth, tears choking her words.

Lydia felt her stomach drop. Suddenly, she was no longer hungry, despite the long day. All she could think of was the danger they were in by staying here. And what of Harmony and her boy? She wished she could get a message to them to stay at the cabin. No one would dare to look for them there. Even if she could get a message to them in time, what about Jewel and her husband, George? And Harmony's family. And the Freemans.

They could all be in danger.

Just then, Rex entered the house with Webster at his side, looking no worse for wear. She quickly filled Rex in. If anyone would know what to do, it would be him. He had a calm, logical manner about him that she had come to depend on in a crisis.

"Don't worry, Lydia," he said when she was finished telling him what Gladys had told her. "I'll call one of the local moonshiners who lives closest to the shack and get the word out."

"What about Jewel and George?"

"George will still be at work. I'll get a message to him to spend the night elsewhere. And I'll have him contact Jewel and the kids. Same goes for Harmony's husband. I'll see if we can get one of them to go warn the Freemans."

"What if the Committee torches their houses?" Lydia demanded, trying to think of all possibilities. "Our house, for that matter."

Rex took her hands in his and faced her squarely. "Lydia, we can't prevent people from being stupid. But we can prepare for any event. If need be, we'll rebuild. I'll see to it. I promise."

Although Lydia had only known Rex for a short time, she found that he inspired confidence. Already, she felt better as she rested her forehead on his chest. Then realizing how this must look, she backed away and quickly offered him sweet tea and pound cake. He drank the tea down in a few short gulps and then followed it up with two bites of the cake, making quick work of the snack she had prepared.

Gladys, who had been quiet until now, barely sipped at the cider, then threw up her hands. "This is all good and well for Jewel and Harmony and their families, but what about you, Lydia, and me, for that matter? The Vigilance Committee knows we helped the people on the train. They believe we're responsible for the spread of yellow fever, and they mean for us to pay. They've been by your place already. Twice! I hid in the bushes. These men had pistols and whatever else, I can only imagine." Once again her words slurred with tears, only this time she could no longer contain her fears. She wept openly, head down.

Lydia stood and rushed to throw an arm around the young woman while Rex offered her his handkerchief. For a moment, Lydia exchanged a worried glance with Rex that contained a message: *What do we do now? Where will we go?* Lydia had no family, and any friends she had made over the past few weeks would surely close their doors to her, too fearful to risk aiding the trio.

And Rex. He had his family, but he'd been too proud to ask for their help in the past. It was doubtful that he would do so now. Lydia couldn't even leave the state until things blew over, as Rose had in her time. No, they would have to ride out the storm and pray that winter would come soon, and with it the return of civility.

"What should we do?" Lydia asked, capturing his eyes with hers.

"What I should have done years ago," he said. "Ladies, pack up your things. And bring something for Webster here. Enough for a couple of weeks, at any rate."

"Where are we going?" the two women asked in unison.

"It's time you meet the Hendersons," Rex said. And although he spoke with complete conviction, his eyes held a wariness about pulling at the scab of his memories that he'd have preferred to leave untouched.

"Your family?" Lydia asked warily.

"That's right. My family." For the first time since she'd known him, she saw tears in his eyes. He was going home, and he was taking her with him.

33

From the Archives of Joan Elaine Fields, M.D.:

"Due to unspecified circumstances, we have lost our first female doctor in Waycross, Georgia, and one of the few in the entire United States of America. She has boarded a steamer ship to Annecy, France. It is rumored she has a friend there. Fortunately, we have a new doctor, Doctor Henry Tapper. Please welcome him into our community. This should help abate the issues involved with having a female doctor and should make our male patients feel much more at ease. The wives of The Welcoming Committee are planning an ice cream social on Saturday morning. Join us in welcoming Doctor Henry Tapper to Waycross, Georgia."

PENELOPE J. RUTHERFORD, THE WAYCROSS SENTINEL

The town seemed to be abuzz with activity. The mayor had called a state of emergency, and even the federal government had brought in a health organization to assess the situation and to see that the illness didn't spread to neighboring states. All this, Lydia learned from Gladys as they drove through town dressed in men's clothes.

A half-hour earlier, Lydia had searched through her father's things until she had found his "farming" clothes, as he had called his old overalls. She'd been able to cinch them on the shoulders and roll up the cuffs to make them fit. To finish off the look, she had worn an old straw work hat.

Afterward, she had turned her attention to Gladys, who looked rather smart in an old gray wool sweater of Lydia's father, and a pair of slacks that he had worn in his early days, before Lydia's mother had fed him too well causing him to outgrow them. Gladys had kept her blouse hidden beneath the sweater. On her head, she wore one of Lydia's father's grey caps. Still, it would be hard to hide such femininity. Lydia could at least keep her head lowered so that the straw hat hid her eyes, but Gladys had only a scarf. In this hot weather, it might look odd.

"What to do... what to do...?" Lydia murmured to herself, and then snapped her fingers. Her father had worn a bandana during hay season, as the hay seemed to bother his sinuses. She quickly went in search of a bandana, picking the blue one as it would draw less attention than the red. "Put this over your face."

"What?" Gladys demanded, not at all amenable. "Put it over your own face!"

"Gladys, we need something to hide the fact that you are a... a..."

"Girl," Rex finished for her. "The fact that you're a girl."

Gladys laughed at that, easing the tension they had all been feeling since the terrible news that the Vigilance Committee had not only discovered who was behind the railway caper, but had learned of their forays across the tracks and was set on revenge.

"I feel like a bandit," Gladys said, once the bandana was covering her mouth.

"Here," said Rex, handing Lydia her father's old hunting rifle.

"What's this for?" she asked, handing it back to him.

He shook his head in exasperation. "Don't you ever just do what you're told?"

"No," she said in all seriousness. "It has to make sense. What if everyone did what they were told to do? What if there were no free thinkers left? What then? That's how genocides occur. That's how civilizations are wiped out."

"Good lord, woman," Rex said, nonplussed. He let loose an exaggerated sigh. "Would you please just take this?" Once again, he handed her the rifle.

"I'll look like someone from the Vigilance Committee."

He raised a single eyebrow.

"Ohh... That's what you want, for me to look like one of them?"

He winked, causing her to blush. "Precisely. They're less likely to stop us if they think we're one of them."

Gladys whistled. "Well, you are the sly one. Then let's go before I burn up in this getup."

"What about Webster?"

"He's a hunting dog, right? People will think we're either out hunting or getting into trouble. Either way, we're less likely to be bothered by Bedford and his gang."

He had a point. Now, they just had to make it across town to the Henderson's place. Rex had never said what had kept him and his family apart after the war. Lydia knew that Rex had shell shock. Late the other night she'd awakened to see him pacing out back, in the dark, cigarette in hand, no doubt reliving his demons from the war. But until she knew him better, she'd thought it wise to let him deal with his demons on his own. She hoped that one day she could earn his trust enough to learn what had caused him to become so fractured, so afraid to step back into the community he had left behind before the war. More than that, what had caused him to step away from his family, to disappear into the shadows of civilized life if there ever was such a thing?

"One last question. I don't mean to state the obvious, but–"

"But what, woman?" Rex said, clearly exasperated by her many concerns.

"Won't everyone know it's us in the Ford, since we're the only ones who own one?"

They all looked at each other, no one saying a thing, until Rex finally broke the silence. "We'll just have to hope they think one of the Committee members stole it. Lord knows they have been known to abscond with other people's property when it suits their purpose."

"That they have," Gladys concurred. "Jenny lost her favorite cow when it got loose. Her husband found it out back of the Farber's house, but didn't dare ask for it back. Not with their reputation."

"And don't forget about those five cases of whiskey that went missing from the back of Larsky's truck," Rex reminded them. "Farber sold it on the black market. Never did spend time in prison, even though everyone knew who did it."

Lydia tugged on her overall strap the way she'd seen her father do whenever he was pondering a situation. "Okay, well let's hope you're both right. We'd better get moving," she said, finishing up the last of her packing.

"Everybody ready?" Rex asked as he carried their belongings out to the motor car and filled the trunk with them.

Lydia and Gladys nodded, but Lydia noticed the wayward glance from Gladys, the fear that resided in those wide blue eyes, which surely matched her own. With the motor car packed, they quickly hopped into the Model A as Rex cranked the engine.

"Here goes nothing," Lydia said under her breath. They drove out of the alleyway and were just about to launch onto the unpaved street that bordered their land when Lydia saw the Vigilance Committee pull up with a wagon and a mule. In the back of the cart lay a cord of rope, several shotguns and a couple of unlit lanterns.

"Jesus," Rex murmured so lightly that Lydia wondered if it had been the sighing of the wind instead.

"What do we do?" she whispered.

"We turn around now and we'll draw attention to ourselves. Heads down!" he ordered. "We'll cross the road like we're headin' to town. Got it?"

Lydia's heart fluttered in her chest like a tiger swallowtail or a banded sphinx trapped inside one of those lanterns Bedford had brought with him to do God only knew what. She held tight to the door handle as Rex pressed on the gas and steered away from the house, rushing to get around an oncoming carriage before Bedford and his men could see the bright red motor car and give chase. They needed time... and distance. But the old girl coughed and chugged like a smoker who had seen one too many unfiltered cigarettes.

Please, she pleaded inwardly, *don't stall now.*

Lydia closed her eyes, waiting for the inevitable final hiccup before the Model A died, right then and there, in the street, just as Lydia was about to do should the Vigilance Committee apprehend the trio. But the stall never came. Instead, the motor car gave one final chug then switched gears, the carriage barely missing them.

For one brief moment, Lydia thought they were out of the woods, but before she could celebrate their victory, Webster let out a bark and jumped up. Had he recognized Bedford?

She grabbed the puppy and pulled him beside her. The dog seemed to sense something was amiss and immediately began licking her face.

"I love you, too, Webster," she whispered, hugging the dog to let him know that she wasn't angry.

In her head, she counted to three. As she did, Rex punched the vehicle into gear and turned down one dirt road after another, hoping to lose them, if indeed Bedford and his men had heard the vehicle. Lydia knew that although she might have fooled the sheriff with her line about the motor car being stolen, someone like Bedford was not as likely to lose the scent. Not a man like him. Over a lifetime, he had made many false assumptions about folks around town but had dispensed his style of justice, all the same, a justice that had its roots in race, sex, and religion.

Goosebumps sped up her arms and to her scalp as she fought to keep her straw hat from blowing away in the wind. She held poor Webster so tightly that she finally had to ease up when he whimpered.

At that moment, she thought back to her simple life as the invisible girl and yearned for that anonymity now. How different her life would have been had she remained invisible, but then she might never have met Rex or Gladys. She might never have brought this lovable dog into her home. She would have never known the great courage of Jewel and her family, Harmony and her son. Or even of Sage and She Who Sees Beyond the Veil. There were simply too many people to thank, each enriching her life in immeasurable ways. Unfortunately, Bedford and his men were the price she'd been forced to pay in order to rejoin her community. In the end, she hoped that the admission to this rodeo wouldn't prove too high.

"Hold tight!" Rex cried, taking a corner so fast that for one brief second Lydia feared the old girl would overturn.

Fortunately, the motor car righted at the last minute and they raced down an alleyway that led to the old water tower, where they made another right turn around the pumphouse. Seconds later, they heard Bedford's voice as he urged his horse forward at a gallop followed by the sound of a whip. Despite the summer heat, Lydia shivered, her heart hammering in her chest. It seemed forever before anyone spoke.

"Do you think it's safe to venture out yet?" Gladys said, reaching across and gripping the bench seat in front of her.

Rex paused, as though catching his breath. "We'll never know until we try, but to be safe, let's take the back way to my family's house."

Lydia concurred and soon they were motoring down one residential street after another. At long last, the Henderson home came into view, a sprawling mansion, by Waycross standards. It created an imposing facade of Georgian architecture, complete with colonnades and a wide front porch. To the right of the walkway leading up to it stood a massive weeping willow, and beneath it lay an ancient looking beagle.

"Why did you ever leave this place?" Lydia asked without thinking, and immediately regretted her words when she saw the tight set of Rex's eyes.

"It's a long story," Rex said. "A very long story."

A story Lydia had a feeling they were about to discover.

At that moment, a tall thin man appeared on the porch, rifle in hand. Even at this distance, she could see that he had steely eyes and an air about him that spoke of a man used to having his way and accepting nothing less.

When she looked over at Rex she saw something she hadn't expected. Tears. And what else? Resolve perhaps. Gritty determination to set things right... or to end them permanently?

Truth is, she didn't know.

34

"Baby, baby bumpkin, had a little pumpkin, set it in the river. Ate it for dinner. Spit out a seed. It grew into a pumpkin weed. Filled an entire patch.

Along came a fox, who hid among the hollyhocks. Waited until the pumpkin grew. But sly fox searched for Mouse. Who set up her little house.

Inside the giant gourd, she sat–knitting a child's hat.

Baby, baby bumpkin, fox is gone a'huntin'. Going to get a little mouse, sitting in her little house.

Snip, snap, gone!"

Lydia didn't know why the child's ditty that Rose had written had come to her just now. Perhaps it was because Rex's father, with his hunting dog and rifle, reminded Lydia of that fox. And she wasn't sure if she or Rex were the little mouse. She just knew that she had the urge to pack them all back into the Model A, Webster and Gladys included, and go somewhere, *anywhere*, so long as it wasn't here.

A nudge on her arm caused Lydia to turn. Gladys leaned in

and whispered, "Didn't you say that Rex's parents used to ask members of the church to pray for his safe return home?"

Lydia nodded.

"Then why does his father seem so... so... unwelcoming?" Gladys asked.

Good question. Obviously, there was more to this meeting than Rex had let on, but what that could be, from a family who had once been so tight-knit, was anyone's guess. Before she could ponder it further, a plump woman with a mousy brown braid encircling her head like a wreath came bouncing out of the doorway. Upon seeing her son, she wiped her hands on her apron and came running down the steps to greet him. At that moment, the bonds of mother and son broke the tension and cries of joy and laughter rang out like church bells pealing the hour that her prodigal son had returned home from the war. The one he had brought home with him.

"Rex Aloysius Henderson, you came home. My baby boy is home at last!"

For several minutes, she sobbed into his shoulder, while Rex's father remained glued to the porch, as though a statue set there in perpetuity, made of marble or perhaps stone. The old beagle eyed his master warily, then as if deciding that he too was determined to join in the homecoming, began baying his joy in several long throaty howls before running toward them as quickly as his short, arthritic legs would allow. Soon he joined the mix, running in circles, alternately baying and snuffling as he threw himself time and time again against Rex's legs so as not to be outdone by Rex's mother.

When the pair finally stepped aside to look at each other, Lydia could see that they had been crying, a weakness that Rex's father obviously did not share. Finally, as though in slow motion, the man lay his rifle on the white porch swing and cautiously made his way across the wide expanse of lawn. As he neared, he slowed, if such were possible, and at last, held out his hand in greeting.

"Son." The word hadn't fallen easily from the man's mouth as if he were so unaccustomed to saying it that it tripped on his tongue.

"Father."

Lydia wanted to reach over and shake them both. Didn't they understand the importance of family? She, who knew too well the loss. And yet these two seemed determined to step around each other like two wrestlers in a ring, each sizing the other up. Each determined to best the other.

And then it began.

"Why didn't you come around?" Mr. Henderson growled, his sharp eyes narrowing to slits. "Can't you see how unhappy you've made your mother? To hear that you lived like a hobo when we could have taken you in. Have you no honor? You are a disgrace to our family."

So the shaming had begun.

Lydia had heard of families who did this, who saw life as a combat sport. Who lobbed insults like hand mortars. Still, she was taken aback. She, who had come from a family who supported each other, lifted each other up, loved one another. Now it was her turn to remain rooted like a hundred-year-old cedar, unable to lift even the smallest bough.

Finally, she could take it no more and yelled, "Stop it! Just stop! Look what you two are doing to each other. You're tearing each other apart. Is this what family means to you? Family is love, compassion, caring for one another, wanting the best for each other. This is your *son!*" Lydia cried, her voice catching on the final word. "And this is your *father.*"

Gladys came over and threw her arms around Lydia as she

sobbed at the loss of civility. At the cruelty. What would Lydia give to have her mother and father back? Or her aunt Rose, whom she had loved more than life itself. It was the Rose in her that had allowed her to be brave, to find her way back into the world of the Edwardian Era. Who had allowed her to take chances, to help others, to be herself no matter how other people viewed her, and she had no illusions about that. Most–but not all–viewed her as someone looking to stir things up, to right the old injustices which poked the eye of the bear by suggesting that people treat others as they would want to be treated.

Do unto others as you would have done unto you, she quoted from the Bible.

Slowly, she allowed her tears to dissolve. It was then that she realized all eyes were on her. Rex left his mother's side.

"May I?" Rex asked, and Gladys stepped aside to allow him access to Lydia.

To Lydia's surprise, he lifted her chin and gazed into her eyes. Then, without a word, he pulled her to him and hugged her. Lydia didn't have time to wonder what the others thought.

Finally, after several moments, Rex's father cleared his throat and Rex released Lydia but held onto her hand. "Father, Mother, this is Lydia McAllister and Gladys. My parents, Frank and Elizabeth Henderson."

Lydia knew better than to address either traditionalist by their first name. Instead, she simply said, "Mr. Henderson, Mrs. Henderson."

"Well," Elizabeth Henderson said, lifting her double chin and inspecting the two women carefully in their men's clothing, "I suppose we've made our introductions."

What must she think? Lydia wondered. Whatever it was, Mrs. Henderson was too polite to say, but the set of her mouth and her eyes spoke of the distaste she must feel.

"Why don't we go inside, into the parlor. I can have Mercedes prepare us some tea and biscuits."

Although Frank Henderson eyed the trio warily, Elizabeth seemed just as determined to keep her son close for as long as possible. And though Lydia felt certain that Frank ruled the roost in most situations regarding their son, Elizabeth was clearly in charge now.

As Lydia and the others strode up the steps and entered the foyer, Webster at her side, she couldn't help but peer in wonder, her mouth agape. For years, she had known that the Hendersons were wealthy, but how wealthy she'd never realized until entering their home, or perhaps she should call it a mansion, for that was the truth of it.

Once inside, Lydia's gaze traveled the length and breadth of first the hallway, with its sweeping mahogany staircase, then to the library, a room to the left of the grand staircase with floor-to-ceiling books and a large desk, a stand-up globe beside it. The air smelled of lemon polish, as though it were dusted daily and seldom used.

To her right, double doors opened to a room that could only be described as opulent. A white-trimmed alcove with gray silk curtains framed a chintz chaise. And off to one side, a fireplace showcased a vase of magnolias in a fluted urn that was offset by two wall sconces. The tigerwood floor gleamed so that it looked as though one were walking on glass.

In awe, Lydia turned to Rex to ask the question that she had asked before. Why? But then she knew why. His father was ashamed of his son, but again, why? What had happened that Frank Henderson would not welcome his son home from the war with open arms? Something had festered between them that had left an indelible mark, and yet she was at a loss to understand it.

But Rex made clear he wasn't ready to open up, and definitely not in this setting, so she bit her tongue. Instead, she and Gladys took a seat on the chintz divan Elizabeth proffered. Purposely, perhaps, Elizabeth offered Rex a solitary seat opposite them made of the finest Italian leather. Both Frank and Elizabeth sat in ornate chairs of tufted cream damask. Between them rested a table, possibly Chinese, with a pagoda on one side, a sampan on the other and a bridge in between. All of it left Lydia feeling somewhat breathless. No more than ten minutes prior, she had been on the run from the Vigilance Committee and now–for the moment, at any rate–she felt positively safe, if not otherworldly, at the sharp turn life had taken. But isn't that precisely what had happened when she'd first met Rex?

They had barely sat, Webster at Lydia's feet, when Frank Henderson said, "Let's go for a walk, son."

The tone he used felt ominous to Lydia. Her first instinct was to protect Rex, and yet she knew that until the two men spoke their piece, there would *be* no peace. She had to trust that Rex's father loved his son enough to temper his reaction. Still, tension settled like a storm cloud, but finally, Rex rose and his father followed.

"I suppose it's time we talked," Rex agreed.

Elizabeth fussed with the pitcher of mimosa that her maid had brought in, followed by a tiered glass dish of tiny canapes and pastries, and a bowl of fresh strawberries. Lydia wondered if she had always done this–smoothed the edges between father and son.

"So, Lydia was it... and Gladys? How have you come to know my son? And why are you dressed–"

"As men?" Lydia offered.

The woman reached for a small lemon danish with a pair of silver-plated pincers then paused, hand hovering in the air.

Blinking rapidly, she set the Danish down on one plate, filling each in turn, before handing them to her guests.

"It's a long story," Lydia said.

"I have time," Elizabeth said, her green eyes piercing.

Lydia explained as much as she felt she should, then bit down on one of the Danish, finding it delicious despite the tension. She hadn't realized how hungry she was until now.

"I see," the woman said at last. "So, my son is involved in something unsavory once again."

"No, you misunderstand, he has been won–"

"No, *you* misunderstand. You know *nothing* of my son or his past," she hissed, "or you wouldn't have involved him with the Vigilance Committee. He needs calm, order. Not more turmoil. He belongs here, with his mother and father, where he can be looked after."

For some reason, that statement irked Lydia and she set her plate down on the mahogany table.

Gladys, who had been listening to the exchange, fidgeted with her hat that she had removed upon entering. When she noticed Lydia watching her, she sat the hat on the table beside her.

"I don't mean to sound disrespectful–" Lydia began.

"Then don't!" Elizabeth spoke with an edge to her voice.

"But your son is a grown man," Lydia continued. "He should be allowed to make up his own mind how to live."

To Lydia's surprise, the matronly woman laughed as she sat her china teacup onto her lap. "You are young and foolish. You know *nothing* of men or wars. You understand none of what these men go through, what they have seen, what they have done." She nearly spat the final words at Lydia. "They don't need coddling. They need a strong hand."

"They also need someone with a heart."

Elizabeth gasped and fell back in her chair. "How dare you! This is *my* son we are talking about. Mine!"

Lydia felt as though she'd received a physical blow because, the truth is, she didn't know Rex all that well. She certainly didn't know about his past, and he had been circumspect in discussing the war. No, *more* than circumspect. He had shut her out completely where that was concerned. She'd thought it was to protect her, but perhaps it was to protect himself as well. She couldn't be certain.

Frustrated by the direction of the conversation, Lydia worried the corners of the lace napkin with her fingers. She hadn't meant to start an argument, *or* to open old wounds. She had merely hoped to learn more about Rex. Now, she had simply opened a door into a maze of rooms that she felt certain would lead to still other rooms, some of what she discovered making sense, some of it making no sense.

For instance, what had caused the estrangement between parents and son in the first place? What had Rex done that could have been considered unforgivable to his parents, so much so that it had created this huge rift? She knew the result–that he had left the prison of his years in the Spanish-American War behind. But what had happened to cause him to want to disappear into a new life? That's what was unclear. And what had led him to be in the Spanish-American War in the first place in a family of such wealth? There were so many unanswered questions, and yet she was afraid to ask them here, with this woman who was clearly angered at any or all mention of her son. She held a proprietary air to her son, as though she owned him. It was an odd relationship, one that went against Lydia's upbringing of such good people as the McAllisters.

"Let me start over," Lydia said, looking to Gladys for support. "You're right. I don't know your son all that well, but I would like to know him. And I also believe in second chances."

Elizabeth deflated like a balloon flower after a hard rain. And yet she just as quickly picked herself up and straightened her spine, then gave just the briefest of smiles to both Lydia and Gladys.

"I do too. That's why I'm grateful that you brought my son home. We *do* love our son. Hopefully, one day he will understand that and maybe even come to appreciate it."

For the first time since Lydia had arrived at this Georgian manor, she felt hopeful. At least they were in agreement about that. Each had Rex's best interest at heart. Both women wanted to see him succeed. And if it could be said, she was beginning to feel a closeness to him that had eluded her with other people. It gave her a shiver of pleasure to know he had returned that closeness when they had arrived.

As if to seal their current truce, Mrs. Henderson urged them to take from the tiered tray of canapes and then handed them each a mimosa.

"Well, ladies, drink up," Elizabeth said, lifting her mimosa by way of a ceasefire.

Lydia gulped down the champagne and orange juice, feeling much cooler and more at ease than she had before. She was just about to ask for the canape recipe when she heard the front door crash open and Rex yell from the foyer, "Lydia, Gladys, we're leaving. Get your things. And Webster too."

Seconds later, Rex rounded the corner with his father close at his heels, yelling something that Lydia couldn't make sense of—something about being a deserter. "No son of mine—"

But before he could finish, Elizabeth jumped to her feet and shouted, "Stop! Both of you. Just stop! We have guests."

"We're leaving," Rex reiterated, but his mother was already at his side, his shirt fisted in her hand as the much shorter woman pleaded for him to stay. "I love you, Mother, but I can't be here right now." Then he turned to the others. "Lydia? Gladys?"

The pair jumped to their feet, Lydia feeling as though a whirlwind had swept in and swirled up a cloud of dust that would choke them if they didn't leave this second. Rex pried his mother's fingers from his clothing and held her fists together, then kissed her on her forehead to let her know how much he cared. Then, as kindly as possible, he sat his mother in the damask chair and took Lydia's hand, Gladys at her side.

"Let's go!" he said, sweeping past Frank Henderson, who appeared flummoxed, clearly not used to seeing his son stand up for himself.

They were almost to the motor car, the beagle howling to see Rex go, Webster nearly forgotten in the melee. Fortunately, he had scrambled to his feet, claws scratching at the floor as he raced behind them and followed them to the car, both dogs barking.

"Wait!" Gladys yelled. "I forgot my hat! I'll just be a minute."

Before Lydia could protest, she was gone.

"Get in!" Rex barked as he ran around front to turn the hand crank.

"Stop!" Lydia grabbed his hand and forced him to look at her. "What happened out there?"

"It's *my* business," he said, his eyes wild with determination to be free from the piercing eyes of his father who stood on the porch, seething.

"Well, you've made it mine."

He went back to cranking the engine and stopped as the motor car sputtered to life.

"Your father said you deserted your post."

Rex stopped, stiffened. "You heard that?"

Lydia nodded and watched as he licked his lips.

"It's not what you think," he said, all the frustration and anger gone. "I had to go. To help a friend. He was in trouble. I had no choice."

"There's always a choice," she said, her tone softening.

He offered up a humorless laugh. "You would think so, wouldn't you? But sometimes there are no good choices. Sometimes there are just two bad choices. And sometimes you pick the lesser of two evils."

Lydia threw up her hands. "You're making no sense."

"My friend from the war–his girl was leaving him for someone else. He flipped out. Left his post. Said he was going to kill her or himself. I couldn't let that happen. Hell, I'd known the guy since kindergarten. What was I supposed to do? Let him end up in prison for life, or dead? What kind of a man would I be if I let that happen?"

She saw the pain of loss in his eyes, of love for a friend. "So you went after him." He nodded. "And then?"

"I ended up in the brig. The military gave me a dishonorable discharge as a deserter." His eyes drifted to where his father, and now his mother, stood on the porch, Elizabeth fretting her hands together over the son she loved, Frank still angry at the son who had dishonored the family name. At that moment, Gladys came through the doorway of the mansion, offered what looked like apologies to Rex's parents as she passed the pair and ran down the stairs.

"Why did they make a show of wanting you home then?" Lydia asked, rushed for time to find the answers to her burning questions. "Why did they ask the church to pray for your safe return?"

"Why do you think?" he said, turning back to her, their eyes lingering. "They didn't want to lose their standing in the community."

"You mean no one knew about the dishonorable discharge?"

"No one but my parents."

Just then, Gladys appeared at their side panting, hat in hand. "What now?" she asked, taking in the two, her eyes wide with the realization that something had happened between them during her absence.

Lydia looked to Rex for answers.

"We go back home and we stand strong," he said, an edge of futility in his voice.

Lydia exchanged a worried look with Gladys who seemed to feel exactly as she did... frightened. But Rex was right. They couldn't run any longer. Rose had done that and her life had ended poorly. No, they would need to show they were united. And they would need support. Lydia thought of the ladies in her sewing guild... of what amazing women they were. She would call them. Together, they would think of a way to calm the waters before the town erupted into a torrent of fear and retaliation. They could help her, if anyone could.

35

From the Archives of Joan Elaine Fields, M.D.:

"Who was it who said, 'All the world's a stage and all the men and women merely players?' Ah, yes. Shakespeare. That poet of poets whose words seem as true now as then.

"I have learned that I am dying, as we all have been since birth, only some of us are closer than others to the Great Divide, or perhaps it's the Great Divine. Or perhaps nothing at all. Perhaps merely the Great Void. The Vast Unknown. And so it is that I leave you with one last word about fashion.

"We come into the world naked, and we leave it so, nothing save our bones to remind us that we once lived. Once loved. Once hoped and dreamed and cared. Everything else is the flotsam of life. The detritus that gets in the way. If only we had known from the beginning that this is so, we may not have fought for wealth, status, the 'material' things in life and instead have seen the fabric for what it was, for what it should have been—a means to draw us closer, to connect. To be seen for who we are.

"And so, it is with regret that I say adieu and wish you all just one

AUNT ROSE'S FINAL FASHION FACT

As so often happens in life, Lydia didn't need to call her new friends in the sewing guild. Because, as the motor car rounded the corner onto Main Street, Rex slammed on the brakes at the sight of a gathering crowd, but not in time to avoid running into the back of a donkey cart filled with apples. Like tiny ball bearings, they cascaded down the sides and back of the cart, bouncing onto the ground. Within seconds a cry of glee arose from the crowd and the cart was soon surrounded, people filling their pockets with juicy red apples.

Rex leaned out the driver's side window and shouted to a woman with a small child who had bent down next to the motor car to pick up a rolling apple. "Ma'am, what's going on? Why the crowd of people?"

She filled her apron first, then stood. "Haven't you heard? No merchandise is allowed in or out of the city. The General Store is nearly empty. Everyone is grabbing anything they can."

Before she could say more, first one man, then another, leaped into the back of the apple cart and began throwing apples to the crowd. Soon people were pushing each other out of the way, at times coming to blows over the precious cargo. The driver of the lorry jumped out and tried to climb onto the cart to stop the theft, but a scruffy-looking character with an overgrown beard and hair that curled at his ears pushed him back, whereupon he landed in the crowd and was set on his feet with an apology from one of the men who had caught him.

"I'll be ruined," the driver of the apple cart cried. But few were listening.

Lydia turned in time to see a bread truck pull up behind them with the same results. Within moments, the driver was on the ground with a bloody lip and a swollen eye. Loaves flew from the back of the cart to cries of delight from the crowd, anguish for the baker.

Determined to do something to stop the wholesale theft, Lydia stood on the black leather seat of the motor car and began shouting, but no one was listening. They were too busy looting the line of carts that had brought local wares to sell in the cash and produce starved city as nearly all industry had come to a standstill.

"Stop! Line up and take turns. We need to pay for the wares!" Lydia admonished.

"How can we pay for anything?" growled a surly woman whose lumpy body and lined face spoke of a hard life. "The banks are closed and most of the businesses are shuttered. We have families to feed." Then she turned, pushing and shoving her way toward the bakery cart.

Lydia sat back down and turned to Rex, feeling a renewed panic as the Model A began to rock back and forth until she thought it might topple. "What should we do?"

From the back seat, Gladys reached over and said, "Well, I know what we *can* do to stop this!"

She jumped to her feet and gave the loudest whistle Lydia had ever heard. Then, hand on hips to make herself appear larger, Gladys yelled, "All of you, just SHUT UP!"

The crowd seemed stunned by the sheer impoliteness of her words because, like crickets on the still night air, their constant chirping fell into instant silence at the surprise intruder.

"Now!" she cried. "Molly, I know your family. And you, Jules. And you, Timothy. Shame on all of you!"

Lydia felt a thrill of excitement, for she was indeed right to have trusted Gladys, the woman who, for all her flightiness, had gumption. A gumption that Lydia had tried hard to emulate.

"But you!" Here Gladys pointed at a very well-heeled man in a gray, three-piece suit with silk cravat and a pearl-handled cane. He turned, as though searching for someone behind him. "You're a banker. Open up the bank. Give people what they need to live until we overcome this crisis."

He scoffed at the very idea that such a young woman as Gladys would dare to tell him what to do. It was clear he would have none of it. So, before he could disappear into the crowd, Lydia stood, adding her voice to the choir.

"Mr. Taylor," Lydia said, giving him his due, "you only need to give people enough per family to feed them and keep them afloat until this ban passes and business resumes. We're not asking for anything that is not ours."

A chorus of "yes" and "that's right" rang through the crowd as all eyes turned to the banker, awaiting an answer. It was then that the mayor, who had pulled up in his carriage at the far side of the crowd, stood on the bench seat of his vehicle and waved his top hat to get everyone's attention.

"You heard the lady, open the bank!"

The banker stroked his goatee as though seeking a way out of this predicament. Finally, he lifted his cane and said, "It's my duty to protect the bank. So, if you will excuse me."

As he tried to leave, someone moved to block his escape.

"Step aside," he cried, lifting his cane once more in warning.

The mayor, who had been watching the ordeal, held up a document. "Mr. Taylor, by order of the federal government, you are hereby ordered to open the bank."

"You are mad," the banker fumed. "You know as well as I do that there would be a run on the bank if we opened it now."

"According to their savings, each family has been guaranteed up to thirty dollars to equal the average monthly wage. We will honor that." The mayor left no room for discussion.

"And how do you suggest I implement that?" the banker cried, clearly angry at the suggestion. "If I open the doors, I'll be mobbed."

"The federal government has sent troops to keep order. We've asked for help from neighboring banks so that we can streamline the process."

"What about my bread?" the bakery salesman yelled. "Who will pay for that?"

"And my apples?" the man from the apple cart called.

"We will see that you are reimbursed," Mayor Blake Thornesby said. "Until then, you are all to disassemble. The doors to the bank will open in an hour by order of the federal government, and we will set up a farmer's market for anyone needing food supplies. In the meantime, the mercantile will be restocked as soon as the ban on the borders is lifted. Now, until then, go back to your homes."

Although a mutter of discontentment rose from the crowd, the townsfolk seemed to recognize the wisdom in the mayor's words. With the crowd quickly dispersing, both Lydia and Gladys sat back down and waited until the road was clear and they could move forward.

"What now?" Lydia said, once they were on their way.

"We go home," Rex said, "and hope that the Vigilance Committee hasn't decided to pay us a visit."

* * *

When they arrived at the old Victorian, after having dropped Gladys off at her apartment, Lydia viewed the old girl through fresh eyes. For years the Victorian had simply been a home, but now it was more than that. It was a refuge against a world gone mad. Yet she mourned her poor neglected flowers, wilting in the heat of the day.

Recognizing her look of forlorn, Rex said, "Don't worry, Lydia, I'll water those."

"Thank you, Rex." Lydia felt exhausted from the day's trek, feeling as though she had been through a war and was only now returning home. Still, after all she had experienced over the course of the past few days, she wanted nothing more than to be close to her aunt who had understood the trials of a city on edge.

While Rex watered the garden, Lydia fed Webster, then changed out of her men's clothing and into something more suitable before making the slow trek upstairs to the attic. As she had before, in what seemed a lifetime ago now, she looked at the trunk with its strange French markings and wondered whose it was and where it had come from. Surely, if it had been Rose's, she would have told them she'd traveled to France. No. It must be someone else's, but whose?

Next, she turned to the trunk. Over the past few weeks, she had removed each dress, one by one, and sewed them anew. Turned them into modern dresses that brought attention to an otherwise boring person... Lydia.

She opened the lid. One dress remained in a faded blue box with no markings. She pulled it out of the trunk and turned it over. On the front was the Eiffel Tower, and the words "Ooh La La" in a series of feathery loops. Lydia frowned and set the box on the dusty floor. Carefully, she opened it. Her heart beat loudly in her chest at the sight. She couldn't have been more surprised than if she had opened the box and a cloud of butterflies had flown out.

A wedding dress.

But *whose* wedding dress?

Lydia stood and walked over to the mirror, then lifted the dress to frame her body. Oddly, it fit perfectly. It had beautiful seed pearls on the bodice and simple straps. But it was the skirt that amazed her as it was made of *moire*, a watery silk fabric with flowers and bows weaved so finely into it that the dress fairly shimmered despite the slight discoloration of age.

"But Rose never married," she whispered to the woman in the floor-length mirror, its wavy lines only adding to the feeling Lydia had of walking into a fairytale.

She heard footsteps, and just as she turned Rex appeared at the opening of the attic, mouth agape as he took in her appearance. For a moment, they stood there like that, each taking in the other.

Finally, they both began speaking at once, then said, "You first." "No, you." Laughter eased the tension.

Rex said, "I'll go first. You look stunning. Is that your mother's dress?"

"No," Lydia said, holding it tightly to her, as though it might disappear if she moved even slightly. "I have a picture of my mother in her wedding gown on the fireplace. It wasn't nearly as lovely as this."

"I should say," he said, with more enthusiasm than perhaps he had meant to. "Then whose is it?"

Lydia shrugged. "I don't know. Rose never married. But if she had, she would have loved this gown. She would have looked beautiful in it," she added with sadness at the thought that her aunt had died... had never been able to express true love openly.

"I came up here to ask you about the water spigot. I think it was turned off somehow."

"Oh, right," she said, casting aside the lovely gown for now. "I'll show you where the main is located."

They were almost to the doorway when she stopped, remembering her earlier conversation with Rex about his friend leaving his post, and Rex rescuing him only to be tagged as a deserter. "What happened... long ago, during the war...? You did what you thought was right at the time."

"I let my men down. Someone died because of my carelessness." Through the light of the transom, she saw tears glisten in his eyes. "I understand why my father can't forgive me."

She took his hand and held it between both of hers. "But don't you think it's time you forgive yourself? You'll never be truly home until you do."

His eyes scanned the floor and he wiped away tears with his index finger. "I would like to come home. For good." He looked into her eyes, searching.

"This is your home," she said. "Welcome back."

He hung his head and mumbled a brief thanks, then looked her squarely in the eye. For several moments, they stood there like that until Webster broke the spell as he scrambled up the stairs.

They were just about to go downstairs when Rex stopped her and pointed to a faded slip of paper on the aged wooden floor of the attic. "What's that?"

Lydia turned and frowned. "That wasn't there before. It must have fallen off the dress."

She walked over and bent to pick it up. Through the transom window, a ray of light shined like a beacon, clearing away the dust and cobwebs, the gloom. With one deft motion, she held the note to the light and read it. The words were in French.

"What do you think they mean?" she asked Rex, who had come to stand beside her.

"My French is pretty rusty, but I think it says 'to my love, on our wedding day'. Do you know anyone who was married in

France?"

Lydia shook her head while Rex merely shrugged. Surely, Doc Henry would have said something the other day if he and Rose had married.

"Is it really that important that you know whose dress it is? I mean it *has* been here for years."

And it was true. Lydia had never bothered to search the attic. She had always been too busy keeping up with the rest of the house on her own to spend any time in the attic.

"Hmm," she said, tucking the faded note into her pocket.

"I'd say we have enough to worry about, Miss Lydia," Rex said, surprising her by using her formal title, "wouldn't you?"

After the mounting tension of the day, she had to laugh, then grew more serious. "What will we do if the Vigilance Committee returns?"

"We'll cross that bridge when we come to it. Still, I hope you don't mind that I've been collecting your daddy's guns and rifles, just in case. Do you know how to use them?"

"Not well," she admitted.

Although her father had taken her out with him hunting once or twice as a child, she had never been a good hunter, altogether too squeamish. Besides, she preferred to root for the animals that she saw as her friends rather than as supper. To her relief, her father had soon seen her as a distraction and had left her home. No, her joy came from creative pursuits: the garden, design, and from all things of an artistic nature. Truth be told, as a child, she had copied her aunt's exploits, had pretended to write columns, stories, and had drawn everything imaginable. People, animals, architecture. She had even designed her own fashion as was evidenced by the drawings she'd stuffed into the nooks and crannies of the attic.

Until Rex spoke up, she'd almost forgotten he was there,

she'd been so lost in thought.

"At any rate," he said, "let's hope we never have to use your daddy's guns, but if we do, we'll have them available."

For some reason, she worried that by merely having them they might invite trouble. But she believed Rex to be of sound judgment, so she simply said, "Let's hope."

Because hope was all they had.

36

From the novel, *The Great Unraveling*, by Joan Elaine Fields, M.D.:

"Coco Chanel, one of the most noted designers in current history, was born to an unwedded mother, whose family paid the father, Albert Chanel, to marry her. Ms. Chanel's mother died of tuberculosis when Coco was twelve years old, whereupon the young designer was sent to the Aubazine Convent in Central France, which operated an orphanage. It was here, she learned to sew. At age eighteen, she left the orphanage, her destiny forever changed."

For the rest of the day, Lydia stewed about the wedding dress, wondering who it had belonged to, and why France? In the meantime, she called Gladys and was happy to discover that she was leaving for her sister's house on the outskirts of town. Her brother-in-law would act as escort. She had promised to call Lydia the very moment she arrived safely.

Outside, the traffic flowed nonstop, buggies traveling to and fro as the townsfolk hurried to the bank to queue up for what monies were coming to them, afterward, lining up at the outdoor market to collect whatever food was available. Fortunately, Lydia had a thriving vegetable garden, and in the past had paid Mr. Holt, a neighbor three doors down, for any spare venison, which she canned, so she was well stocked. Plus she had a chicken coop out back. Better to allow those in need to get what they could and for her to stay put.

Contrary to her expectations, the doctor and the mayor had not called on her and Rex to help with what was quickly becoming a yellow fever epidemic since their return from the scare with Harmony's son. She wondered if they, too, had heard about the Vigilance Committee's threats. If not, she should tell them. That's when an idea came to her.

It was nearing supper time when Lydia had come up with a plan that she hoped to implement on her own. She had just started to get supper around when Rex entered, appearing hot and sweaty from a day outdoors.

When Lydia told Rex her idea, he said, "You can't go alone."

"And why not?" she demanded, used to her independence.

"Because it's not safe. If you have forgotten, the Vigilance Committee is still out there looking for you. Better that the two of us stay together than you go it alone."

Although she knew he was right, it bothered her that she couldn't move freely in her own hometown without fear of reprisal. Where were the days when people had felt free to leave the front door unlocked, kids running loose until suppertime? It seemed that the entire town had closed up like a hibiscus flower, only to reopen, abuzz with activity until the next calamity sent them indoors.

"So what do you suggest?" Lydia asked.

"We leave after supper."

"After supper it is."

That settled, Lydia made quick work of the meal, not even bothering to wash the dishes before they left. She worried about leaving Webster at the house. No telling what might happen if the Vigilance Committee returned, but he appeared worn out from their long excursion, so she placed him outdoors and made certain he had food and water before making their exit.

Fifteen minutes later, with the boxed wedding dress placed in the trunk of the motor car, they made the crosstown drive. Lydia waited for Rex to pull up to the curb of Doc Henry's home before disembarking. The doc's office was built on the side of his house where he dealt with the less complex matters of the day. Lydia knew she was pulling at straws, but if anyone might know what had happened to Rose during the year she had disappeared, it would be Henry.

Her nerves on edge, Lydia traipsed ahead of Rex to the door of the stolid little house that was nothing like the mayor's mansion. This was a sturdy house with a peaked roof, white, like her own, a green lawn and a stately elm to keep the house cooler in the summertime. Like most other houses in the South, this one had a screened porch for nights when it was too hot to sleep indoors.

Steeling herself, Lydia knocked on the screen door and waited. Minutes later, the shortish man appeared, looking different now in his after-hours attire–a plain tan shirt with a dark pair of cotton trousers held up by suspenders. The change in him since she'd last seen him was striking. His skin sagged and his eyelids drooped, and his eyes were red and swollen from fatigue.

"Glad you caught me at home, Miss Lydia," Doc Henry said, ushering them in. He offered them sweet tea and some cookies that one of his patients had baked for him, but Lydia politely declined. It had finally dawned on her that until she knew what caused yellow fever, everything was suspect. She thought of the mimosa she'd had earlier and the food she'd eaten at the cabin. Hopefully, whatever the dreaded disease, it wasn't foodborne.

As if reading Lydia's concern, the doctor said, "I'm fairly convinced this disease is not a foodborne illness. I've hired a secretary to take notes as we go, and I can connect no food or handling of food with yellow fever. Some doctors have voiced concern that the disease may be airborne, but the truth is, we really don't know. Most of the persons in question have had no contact with other sufferers, so more and more I believe it is *not* transmitted through human contact."

Lydia fanned herself, sweat rolling down her chest and back.

Seeing her like this, the doctor stood. "I'm sorry. The house has been closed up with me gone so much of the time. Why don't we go out back."

He led them through to the rear porch where a round table with four chairs awaited beneath the shade of a giant sycamore tree. Once they were settled and feeling a bit cooler, he added, "In all cases, yellow fever seems to abate as soon as the weather turns colder."

"If the town doesn't blow apart before then," Lydia said without thinking.

The two men exchanged nervous glances.

"Precisely," Doc Henry said, rubbing his finger on the rim of his glass in a tireless motion. "We have to pray for rain... and cold weather."

"We're nearing the cold season," Rex offered as he tapped the bottom of his cup against the red plaid tablecloth.

"That we are," the doctor agreed, "and it can't come soon enough for my liking."

Normally, Lydia had loved summers. It was a time for

tending the garden and canning, for seeing more of those who spent their winters indoors through the leaded panes of her window, or as she weeded. It was as though the world slept all winter and then awoke, reminding her she was alive, that she had survived another winter alone.

Now, perhaps, she would no longer feel so alone in wintertime. She envisioned evenings spent around the fire with Webster beside her, and Rex working by candlelight on some project that he was unable to do during the daytime. Together, she and Rex could listen to the radio, keep up with the latest news or listen to one of the melodramas put on by Westinghouse, or Texas Star Theater. Or perhaps they could simply listen to the phonograph. But first, they had to survive the summer.

Lydia spent the next twenty minutes telling the doctor what had transpired over the past several days, and the doctor did the same, revealing that he had been called out on so many cases that he could no longer handle the workload. Apparently, according to Doc Henry, he had tried to contact her and Rex to seek help with the afflicted, but they had been on the move so much, he hadn't succeeded.

"Fortunately, the state is calling in doctors as far away as Atlanta to come help so you will no longer be needed. Many are here already, thank the good Lord. We've had twenty-three deaths so far, and literally a hundred or more ill. It's the worst year on record for yellow fever."

For the first time that night, the doctor appeared defeated as he ran his hands through his thinning hair. "I'm sorry. I'm just tired. Was there anything else you wanted to talk to me about?" he asked, clearly looking to rest now.

Seeing her window of opportunity closing, Lydia said, "I have to ask you something, but first I have something to show you." She grabbed the keys to the trunk of the Ford. "Wait here."

Moments later, she returned with the pale blue box she had discovered in the attic chest. Even before she opened it, the doctor paled.

"You recognize this box?" she asked, excitement causing her fingers to tingle. "Was it Rose's?"

He paused, running his finger along the rim of his glass. Then finally, he nodded forlornly.

"How?" she demanded.

"Because I gave it to her," he said with a sigh.

Lydia felt as if the crimson sun that lay on the horizon was mocking her. How could she not have known? Why would her aunt, who had shared almost everything with Lydia, have refused to confide this monumental secret?

"Why? How?" Lydia felt as if her head were spinning. "Start from the beginning."

The doctor bit his lips as though pondering how much he should tell her. Then, as if coming to a decision, he pushed his glass away and faced her.

"We were in love."

"Then why didn't you marry her–I mean openly? No one knew about you two, least of all her family." Lydia hadn't realized how vehement she sounded, accusatory.

Doc Henry's face appeared ashen. "You have to understand. By that time she had already developed a reputation in town. There was a trial. Against a black man accused of rape."

Lydia recalled that time but hadn't known about the trial, only the whispers, the stares. Her mother would have made sure she hadn't heard a word of it.

"Everyone knew the charges were trumped up to prevent a white man from going to jail for rape. The black man would have been convicted if she hadn't helped him." He paused, eyes moistening. "But as you know, helping the downtrodden is an unforgivable sin in this town. And helping a black man, even worse."

"So you couldn't marry. But why not move somewhere else where no one knew you?" she demanded, hands splayed. "None of this makes sense."

"By that time, the medical community had already taken away her license. Medical malpractice they said. But you know that's not true. She pleaded for me to step in and take over the practice here in Waycross. That way she knew the people in this town would receive good care, but there was a proviso in the contract that I would stay a minimum of a year or I could be sued. We hadn't counted on..."

Here, he looked away, his eyes red-rimmed, whether from fatigue or sorrow at the memory, Lydia couldn't be certain. She only knew that a piece of the puzzle was still missing. Why had Rose left this man for an entire year when she obviously loved him?

"What hadn't you counted on?" she asked as softly as possible, hoping to lure him back to the topic at hand.

Swallowing hard, he turned to face her once more. "We hadn't counted on the fact that she would become pregnant."

Lydia felt as though the air had left her lungs, as yet another piece of the puzzle fit neatly in place.

"Once things had calmed down," he continued, "we had planned to be married, but we had already waited so long." He drowned his sorrows in the last of his sweet tea.

"What happened to the baby?" Rex asked.

Doc Henry wiped his brow before answering. "Her name is Joan Elaine Fields. It was Rose's idea–to give her a different last name. Joan is amazing and beautiful, though as her father I may be a bit partial."

"Wait! Rose gave birth to a child? How? Where?" Lydia

looked around the spartan backyard with its carriage house that faced the alleys and at the beleaguered hostas, as though the girl might materialize from thin air.

"She lives with my sister in France. Annecy to be precise."

Lydia couldn't have been more shocked if he had told her he had two heads. Feeling spent, suddenly, she fell back in her seat, grateful to Rex who took her hand and gave it a reassuring squeeze. In the intervening moments, Lydia counted out the years on her hand. Joan Elaine would be ten years old. The thought gave her a flicker of excitement. Yet, like a fire that had sparked, it was just as readily quelled.

"Why did Rose return here? She would never have left her child behind. Never."

The doctor gave a wry laugh, lacking any warmth or humor. "Because she was dying. She wanted her child to have a happy life, and she knew Joan would have it with my sister, Bertrande. She's a wonderful woman, and she loves little Joan."

"Joan..." Lydia rolled the name off her tongue. "Joan. I have a cousin."

"That you do," the doctor said, appearing more tired than ever before.

Rex squeezed her hand as if to remind her that the doctor needed his rest after weeks of little sleep. Besides, she had learned what she had come for. There would be time, once the weather cooled, to learn more.

"I've kept you too long," she said, rising. "Thank you so much for telling me all this. I have a cousin!" she said in wonder, a smile forming on her lips unbidden. She still had many questions, but they could wait. She picked up the faded blue box feeling a deep abiding love for her aunt, and for these two new people in her life.

The doctor walked them around the side yard to the waiting

motor car. Just as Lydia was about to get in, she stopped.

"Why did you have to keep your relationship a secret when Rose returned to Waycross? Or better yet, why didn't you just leave at that point?"

He sighed and put his hands in his back pockets as though wishing to rid himself of the awful memories. "Because the Vigilance Committee sent out word the minute Rose returned home that anyone who 'consorted' with her would be punished. Rose was protecting me. Fortunately, I was able to see her often because of her illness. And we found other ways."

Lydia thought that over and frowned. "But that still doesn't answer my question. Why didn't you simply leave at that point? Your contract would have been up by that time."

"True." He looked past her, chewing on his upper lip.

"But?"

He sighed and stared at her with penetrating blue eyes. "Because she couldn't leave *you*. For all intents and purposes, you were her daughter. Your mother was a lovely woman, God bless her soul, but she had a very busy life in this town, as you know. Rose filled in, took up the slack. And, well... she loved you."

Lydia's throat tightened and she fought back tears. Of course. Rose had loved her. And she had shown it, right until the end.

"Thank you," Lydia said, kissing the doctor on the cheek. The man turned a deep shade of crimson, but she had seen the fierce gleam of pride, despite all that he had been through for Rose. "One last question. Did you two marry and were my parents there?"

He shone with an inner light. "That we did. It was the best day of my life." Before she could interrupt, he added, "And yes, your parents were there." As Rex started the motor car and hopped in, Doc Henry shut Lydia's car door, fatigue evident in the stiffness of his movements.

As they drove away, Lydia peered back and saw the doctor standing on the wide stretch of lawn, his hand raised in farewell. Lydia had a feeling she would be seeing a lot more of him from now on. With any luck, he would be stitched into the weave of this family she had cobbled together. Part of a tapestry that would become her new life. And with that, she smiled.

37

From the novel, *The Great Unraveling*, by Joan Elaine Fields, M.D.:

"Even as racism ran rampant in America during The Civil War, First Lady Mary Todd Lincoln employed a Negro dress designer, Miss Elizabeth Keckley. Born in Dinwiddie County, Virginia, in 1818, Elizabeth suffered beatings and sexual assault, leading to the birth of her son, George. Elizabeth was loaned the money to buy freedom for both her and her son. Afterward, she moved to Washington, D.C., where she set up shop as a dressmaker and met Mrs. Lincoln. Her memoir, Thirty Years a Slave *led to public condemnation, and to a shunning, similar to Rose's, for revealing the inner workings of The White House."*

The darkness had settled in like a shroud, a thin veil of fog canvassing the ground. It wisped in circles around Lydia's ankles as she exited the motor car, like kudzu vines seeking purchase of its host plant. Feeling the moist tendrils of the fog, Lydia shivered, eager to be in the house with the lights on.

Rex must have picked up on her altered mood because he said, "Go on ahead. I'll close up here and make sure the garage is locked before heading in." He placed a hand on her shoulder. "Are you going to be okay? I know it's a shock–learning that your aunt had a baby."

"*Has* a child," she amended. "In France."

France seemed so far away. How would she ever be able to see her cousin? Now that she knew the girl was out there, she knew she'd never feel complete until she got to meet her, to hug her, to tell her how brave her mother was, how amazing she had been in the face of danger. She had so much she wanted to tell the girl.

"It will all work out," Rex said, as though reading her thoughts.

"For you too," Lydia said, thinking back on the day and to the dustup with his parents. She squeezed his hand in reassurance.

"I know. But life doesn't always happen the way we hope or plan." He peered down at their clasped hands. "Sometimes it's way worse, and sometimes it's better than we could have ever hoped." His dark eyes captured hers, holding a meaning that made it hard to breathe.

"That it does," she said in a whisper.

For a moment, they stood there in silence, each riveted to the spot inside the garage, the moon highlighting them both. Then the wind picked up, despite the usual stillness of the hour, and the door rattled. They quickly dropped hands, but not before Lydia had seen the glisten in Rex's eyes, the longing that mirrored her own. How her life had changed in the blink of an eye.

"Go on," he urged. "I'll be in, in a minute."

She dipped her head in acknowledgement. Then exited the

garage, and yet the moment she did so, she felt a shift in the weather, a stillness far deeper than anything normal for this time of night. It was as though the earth had yet to breathe in and exhale. And then she felt it. Eyes watching her from the shadows, the moon unable to expose what lay hidden in the waiting darkness. She hurried toward the house, but before she could reach the steps that would carry her up to the back door, she heard a branch break and the sound of crunching leaves.

"Who's there?" she demanded, heart pounding out a dirge that caught deep inside her throat.

Nothing.

She started to turn and once again heard the crunching, but this time the noise sounded like footsteps. A scream lay buried inside her, as she stood, hands trembling, too frightened even to speak much less scream. To her surprise, out popped Webster, tail wagging. She fell to her knees in relief as he smothered her in doggie kisses.

"I missed you too," she murmured, hugging him tight, reassured by his soft fur and warm body. But before she could give him one last pat and get fully to her feet, she heard his soft growl as he stared at something behind her. Her stomach flipped as she turned in time to see Bedford, his beady eyes filled with loathing, the smell of liquor on his breath riding the waves of air in fumes that made her eyes water.

"You did this," he said under his breath. "You brought yellow fever to Waycross. And you... will... pay."

It was then that she saw a sharp glint of steel in his hand and realized his intent. For moments that lingered, stuck in freeze-frame, she watched him, her mind numb with anticipation of what was to come. And then the reel sped up just as the dog's growl turned to a bark. Within seconds, Webster was lunging at Bedford, the sound bringing Rex at a run. Lights flicked on one house over, her neighbor coming to the back porch. Finally, her voice returned and she screamed just as Webster let out a screech of pain as metal met flesh. Rex pounced on Bedford, the knife knocked from his hand. She kicked it away, beneath her camellia bush and rushed to Webster who was bleeding and panting. She ripped off a strip of her dress, grateful that the material was old and therefore easier to tear. Then she wrapped it around his midsection, praying that no vital organs had been involved.

Once Webster was cared for, she looked around for something, anything to help Rex in his fight. There, in the waning moonlight, she saw the large stone marker that she had placed next to her aunt's favorite flower. With effort, she was able to lift it. Saying a prayer, she lobbed it at Bedford and heard the sickening sound of stone hitting bone. She would worry about the morals of it later. Right now, she had three lives to save and she took her duty to Rex and Webster seriously because although she was wont to admit it, she had come to love them both, dearly.

For one brief moment, Bedford tried to stand, then teetered precariously before falling onto his knees and to the ground. It reminded her of the Peabody's house when it had fallen to the fire, and of her analogy to the Andalusian horse on its knees before collapsing. Despite everything Bedford had done to her and so many others, she prayed she hadn't killed him, that she had only landed him a lancing blow that would incapacitate him long enough to be taken in by the sheriff.

And her prayers must have been answered, for moments later, the sheriff arrived with lights and sirens on, the neighbor, bless her heart, having called him after hearing the commotion. Soon after, a horse-drawn ambulance arrived to take him to the hospital, the driver giving assurances that he would survive.

* * *

Ironically, Lydia had thought there would be a big showdown between her and the Vigilance Committee afterward, much as it had with her aunt. And yet life could be funny sometimes, the twist and turns taking one in directions never imagined.

Because Bedford, it turned out, had done something unforgivable, even more so than what had happened with Aunt Rose, lo those many years ago. After he had healed, he had gone on to attack the mayor's wife, and that could not go unpunished. Fortunately for the town, he was rounded up and placed behind bars, his trial set for September. No one spoke out on his behalf. *No one.*

Now, without a leader, the other men faded back into the fabric of society, the sewing guild pressuring the other women to withhold any of the creature comforts the men had come to expect until they quit attacking both Lydia and the black community, as well as harassing those who had come down with yellow fever or their families. Maids and housekeepers who kept up the men's homes were encouraged to stay on their own side of train tracks, thereby refusing to cook hot meals, clean house, or provide whatever else that made the men from the Vigilance Committee's lives bearable.

And then, an even funnier thing happened. One brisk morning, winter arrived on a blast of cold air. Dew turned to frost and the creaking wheels of the death carts slowed. Soon, they stopped altogether. Once again, the post office began delivering mail and the trains were allowed in with supplies, the far-off whistle a welcome relief and a reminder that things were returning to normal. The borders were opened and, one by one, the doctors returned to their own practices in other cities. The state of emergency had been lifted and only a few beleaguered troops remained.

Just as suddenly, instead of everyone at each other's throats, the town seemed able to breathe again. People smiled and waved hello. Women, who had heretofore never even noticed Lydia's existence, made a point of calling across the street to her, nudging their husbands to greet her as well. There were times when she wanted to pinch herself.

I am visible. People see me.

For so long, she had lived in the shadows, skirting her former life as if seeing it through a window, her on the outside looking in, hungry for warmth, a meal, family, friendship. Now she had that in Rex, Webster, Gladys, who had returned as soon as the weather changed and was even more in her element than before. Even Doc Henry had begun making routine visits. But she had learned something else about herself. Yes, the town had shunned her all those years ago, but in the end, she had shunned the town as well. Thinking back on it, she realized that despite everything that had happened with Rose, people *had* gradually begun to speak to Lydia again after her parents died, albeit rare. But she had no longer trusted their love, their fury. Like dirty laundry soaked too long in lye, all the color had drained out of her life. She had sought the refuge of home. The words used against her had stacked up like firewood used to heat that laundry. How many others had shared the same fate, rightly or wrongly? Had suffered at the hand of words meant to cut. *Just like those spoken to Rose.* More often than Lydia would care to admit, she had heard titters of laughter and words used against others, even at church. *Fat, ugly, and that nose...* Because if you pointed a finger at others, you didn't have to look at yourself.

Well, she planned to do something about all that, to create a safe place for people who didn't fit into the social norm. For decent people. *Kind* people.

One day, nearly a year after the epidemic had passed, Doc Henry surprised Lydia by calling on her on a Sunday, when she was out back with Rex, seated at a large round wooden table Rex had built for them, with chairs to go around, an overhead arbor drenched with wisteria to protect them from the sun. They were sharing mint juleps from a cut-glass pitcher with matching glasses. Lydia had taken an old chipped teapot–one that was especially dear to her as it was her aunt Rose's–and filled it with apricot roses and lime hydrangeas.

Having tried her front door and getting no response, the doctor had ventured to her gate and yelled across it.

"Who could that be?" Rex asked, but Lydia recognized the voice instantly.

"We're back here, Doc!" she called, jumping up and running inside to get another glass for their visitor.

But as she descended the steps bordered by a large gardenia bush, and turned toward the patio, she paused. Doc Henry hadn't come alone. For an instant, Lydia was uncertain who the young visitor might be, but when the girl turned, Lydia felt a welling in her heart and in her eyes, for there could be no mistake. The eleven-year-old girl with beautiful long black hair was Joan, Rose's daughter. Lydia didn't know what to do–to run to the girl who was quickly becoming a young lady, open arms, perhaps scaring her in the process, or to stand back and wait for the girl to come to her.

In the end, she did neither. She walked over to Joan and bent down slightly.

"Hello," she said. "I'm your mother's niece."

Epilogue

Lydia, I wrote this for you, so that one day you would understand everything that happened and why. They say a woman has only two loves, her husband and her child. Well, I have three, because of you. You will always be the light of my life. When I was alone in the world, you helped make me stronger than I am, more heroic. With you at my side, I wasn't afraid. You will always be a daughter to me, even after death.

With love, your aunt Rose

On a warm summer afternoon, with a breeze blowing that gave off the scent of roses that grew on the arbor Rex had designed for her, Lydia said: "I do." In the beautiful moire wedding gown that Harmony had helped her repair, Lydia stood beside the man she loved, Webster at her side. Looking on were Gladys, Harmony and her family, Jewel and her family, and all the women from the sewing guild.

Rex's family had arrived late and appeared awkward in the backyard setting, no doubt wondering why Lydia and Rex hadn't chosen the more opulent setting of their home. But for at least this gathering, they were gracious enough to bite the words that were surely on their tongues. Lydia felt grateful for small mercies.

Her eyes drifted to Dottie. The woman always bore a smile, no matter the circumstances, and those had been harsh, now that her husband was in prison. But fortunately, the women from the sewing guild had restored Lydia's faith in humanity, for they had sounded the clarion call to the members of the church, who had then rallied around Dottie, offering food, help with the yard, and she had even been given a job. Gladys had seen to that. Dottie was now an official switchboard operator at AT&T. Lydia couldn't help but smile. Yet, watery tears formed too, for she wished her mother and father could have been here. And her aunt Rose. And yet she had Doc Henry and Joan. Another reason to be grateful.

Right before the wedding, Joan had arrived with Doc Henry at her side. Lydia had run to greet them. To her surprise, she noticed that the left lamp on the doc's carriage was broken.

Just like the one Jewel was driving when she picked up family members from the train.

Goosebumps trailed Lydia's arms. "You old dog," she said when she saw the amused look on Doc Henry's face.

"We all have our secrets," he said with a sly smile.

Lydia laughed, then turned to Joan, who presented Lydia with a box that she had been patiently holding. Lydia gasped, recognizing it from her childhood, and felt a thrill of memory as she fingered the Bald Cypress. Rose had called it her "treasure chest." Inside, she had kept all her baubles. Lydia had wondered what happened to it.

"Go ahead, open it," Joan said, watching her carefully. Slowly, Lydia lifted the lid of the box that had been decoupaged in magazine photos of women's design. Now, more than ever, Lydia understood why design held such a fascination for her. As the lid creaked open, Lydia saw a stack of letters tied up in a faded green ribbon. She undid the ribbon and, with watery eyes, read the contents within: Aunt Rose's Fashion Facts.

"Thank you. I will treasure them forever," Lydia had said, and she would.

Now, as she gazed at her husband and they said their "I dos," she felt happy at last. Yet, once again, she wished her aunt could have been here to witness her joy.

As she kissed her husband's lips, tasting the sweet nectar of his love, she heard a rustle and felt something brush against her leg. She lifted her skirt and was surprised to see a brass safety pin with a piece of material attached. Carefully, with the entire group watching her, Lydia undid the pin and watched as the silk fluttered to the ground. She picked up the square piece of material. Sewn into the fabric in her aunt's flowery scrawl were the words *I will always love you.*

Lydia's throat tightened and she fought back tears.

Maybe she's with me after all.

Acknowledgments

This book began after I read an article from an old newspaper about a "Yellow Fever Train" bound from Florida through the South. It set me on a journey to explore what happens when a town is faced with a pandemic that upsets the balance of a community and sows discord, revealing the divisions among us, as has happened with the current pandemic, Covid-19. I began writing it long before the pandemic. Fortunately, many angels helped to see this book to fruition. First and foremost, to my writers group, Laine Stambaugh and Elaine Stec. Thank you for all your insightful comments and ideas. Any mistakes I made in the process are my own.

Thanks especially go to Darrin Brenner, artist extraordinaire, who designed my cover page and who walked me through the intricacies of interior and exterior design as a semi-computer illiterate person, despite my experience as an editor. Thanks also go to Sara Rolat, who did the proofreading for *The Great Unraveling*.

And thanks to the many writers I have had the good fortune to work with over the years. They have helped me not only become a better editor, but a better writer. Anything I have learned, I have learned because of them.

Special thanks go out to Natasha Kern for allowing me to work with such wonderful writers and who taught me to hone my skills in the art of storytelling.

Last, but not least, thanks to my husband, Les Craig, who has put up with years of long hours and tight deadlines. I can't thank you enough. I promise to keep my hours to a minimum so that we have time together now that you are retired. And finally to my daughter and granddaughter, Sara and Kaylee Baker, who were gracious enough to read yet another of my books and to provide invaluable critique. Fortunately, they are gracious enough to show true interest and offer great feedback. And lastly to my father and mother, sisters, and brother, who supported me along the way and who encouraged my dream. I could not have done it without any of you. I have worked with many other kind and generous people over the years. You know who you are. You are appreciated more than you will ever know.